SECRETS

a novel

Rebecka Vigus

REBECKA VIGUS

To
Tammy
Enjoy

OPEN WINDOW

Livonia, Michigan

SECRETS

Published by Open Window
an imprint of BHC Press

Library of Congress Control Number:
2017952175

ISBN Number: 978-1-946848-95-6

Visit the author at:
www.bhcpress.com

Also available in ebook

ALSO BY REBECKA VIGUS

MACY MCVANNEL NOVELS
Rivers Edge
Crossing the Line
Sanctuary

OTHER NOVELS
Out of the Flames
Target of Vengeance
Rescue Mountain

SHORT STORIES
Broken Chains
The Heir
Escape (A Macy McVannel Story)
What the Storm Blew In

NONFICTION
So You Think You Want to be a Mommy?

POETRY
Only a Start and Beyond

CHILDREN'S BOOKS
Of Moonbeams and Fairies

CONTRIBUTING AUTHOR
In Creeps the Night
A Winter's Romance

Dedicated to my grandchildren,
Megan Leesa and Jason Christopher Kline,
may you always be safe.

SECRETS

1 MISS EMILY MEEKS was an institution in town. She had been the librarian for as long as anyone could remember. Her fine mousy brown hair barely reached her shoulders and was sprinkled with gray and her huge grey eyes were hidden behind a pair of gold rimmed glasses. She traded her severe gray dresses for light gray pant suits and always wore a pair of sturdy black shoes, which allowed her to be on her feet all day.

She had a routine you could set your watch by. Every morning at 6:30a.m. she stopped at the Oak Grove Cafe for two eggs over easy with bacon, hash browns and whole wheat toast. She also had tea with cream. The waitresses knew her favorite jam was strawberry. She chatted with the other customers and read the Detroit News. By 7:15 a.m. she knew all the local gossip anyone needed to start their day and walked on to the library. She did her inventory, placed orders and did research for the locals until the doors opened at 9 a.m. Yep, you could set your watch by Miss Emily.

It was a surprise to everyone when the library didn't open one Monday morning. Chief Buck Wise was called and set out to retrace the steps Miss Emily took every morning. The waitresses on the morning shift hadn't seen Miss Emily and were wondering if she was ill. One of them had planned to check on her at the end of the shift. Chief Wise made his way to Miss Emily's, hoping to find she stayed home with a chill.

Miss Emily owned a small house on the edge of town. It was a bit run down, but she kept her flowers well tended and they seemed to take over the yard. Chief Wise radioed to tell them he was going to enter the premises as the front door was wide open.

Although he'd known Miss Emily for as long as he could remember, he'd never been in her little house. He knocked firmly on the door frame and called out, "Miss Meeks, it's Chief Wise. Is everything all right?" Getting no response, he walked slowly into the house.

He could hear the TV blaring. Things were overturned and strewn about. He found Miss Emily slumped in her chair in front of the TV. She'd found horror in her death.

He quickly exited the house and radioed for the coroner. While waiting for the arrival of the coroner he began to walk slowly around the outside of the house, looking for clues, looking for anything, avoiding a return to the scene for as long as he could.

Buck Wise was a veteran of the Detroit police force. He'd seen his share of murder. He was a stocky man about five feet ten inches tall. He worked out regularly while he was on the force. He didn't want to be part of the donut brigade. He took pride in staying fit. His dark brown hair and piercing blue eyes made him attractive in the look of old western cowboys. Those who knew him knew he was a kind and gentle person. He moved his family back to his hometown of Oak Grove to shelter them from murder. It had been seven years ago.

Murder didn't happen in his little town. It was the reason he came back here. He hated the murder, and crime in the city. He wanted a quiet place to raise his family. One where people knew each other and murder just didn't happen.

The most puzzling thing was why anyone would want to kill Miss Emily Meeks. She lived in a small house, making a modest little income as the town librarian. She didn't party or do drugs. She wasn't coming into any money as far as he knew and he knew most everything going on in Oak Grove.

Oak Grove, a small town tucked away in an oak grove with a creek running through it. A few Mom and Pop businesses, made up the one block of downtown. Everyone knew everyone. The big events were the football and basketball games at the Oak Grove High School. Along with the Founders Day Festival wrapped up the excitement in Oak Grove. The biggest crime was finding Seth Rankin stumbling down the street after tying one on at Joe's on payday.

Doc Reed arrived with his young assistant. "What's the story, Buck? Miss Emily have a heart attack?"

"I wish it were so easy, Doc. I'm not sure the kid is up to this. It's not pretty."

"So, you're thinking foul play?" Doc asked.

"I'm not sure what it was. I just know it wasn't natural," was Buck's reply. "I'm going to need to know time of death, too. No one seems to have seen her since last Saturday."

"Lead the way. We'll see what I can learn."

The two men and the assistant entered the small house. All three men were careful where they stepped. None were sure what would turn out to be evidence and what was just rubbish strewn about.

"Somebody was looking for something," Doc mused. "They've emptied every drawer in the house. Can't imagine what Miss Emily had someone would go to this much trouble over."

"Those are my feelings," said Buck. "This was not a random search. Someone was after something specific."

"So, it would seem." Doc looked around. "I'll get Junior to photograph the whole place for you."

"Thanks, Doc."

Buck left the house in Doc's capable hands and headed back to the library. He needed to see if Miss Emily left anything there which would give him a clue to what had happened to her.

2 AT THE LIBRARY, he found the night janitor, Henry Watson, waiting for him. Henry was a grizzled old coot of indeterminate age. He had a slightly stooped stance and a thatch of white hair which looked like it never had a comb run through it. He had worked as a laborer all his life and had ended up at the library.

He refused to open the library until he heard from Miss Emily. There was quite a gathering on the steps. Buck sent everyone home and told Henry Miss Meeks would not be in and he needed to get into the library, but it would not be opened to the public for at least a week.

Mr. Watson was not pleased, but he did not argue with the law. "Don't like this one bit, Chief. Miss Emily'll have my hide if somepin' turns up missing. What in tarnation happened here?"

"I was wondering myself, Henry."

The place had been ransacked. Books were everywhere. Drawers were pulled out of the desk and papers were strewn all over. Henry hurried to the nearest pile and reached to pick them up.

"Don't touch a thing!" Buck shouted.

"What do you mean? Miss Emily will have a fit if she sees this!" Henry exclaimed.

"Better wait until my boys get here and take pictures. They'll need to dust for fingerprints, too."

"Chief, what *is* going on?"

SECRETS

"Henry, Miss Emily was murdered over the weekend. Her house was ransacked, too. I need to know everything you can remember about Saturday."

"Miss Emily murdered. No way. There must be a mistake," Henry muttered. "She was just fine on Saturday. Told me there was some apple pie in the fridge we have in the eatin' area. Then she locked up and left same as usual. Who could have wanted to hurt Miss Emily? She was the kindest soul…"

"It's what I aim to find out Henry. In the meantime, I need to know everything you can remember about working and locking up on Saturday night."

"Well, it was quiet as usual. Don't recall anything out o' the ordinary. I did my cleanin', ate my dinner round 'bout 8 o'clock, the pie was real good, then finished up everythin' and locked up 'bout midnight, and went home. I didn't see no one on the way neither."

"Okay, Henry. You just go on home now. I'll have the boys lock up and we'll post a sign saying the library is closed until further notice. If you think of anything else, you just call me at the station."

"Sure 'nough."

Buck saw Henry on his way, then made the call to have the team sent to the library for fingerprints and photos. He walked carefully to the desk where Miss Emily did her work to see if he could spot anything which might be of help to him.

Henry was right, he reflected she was the kindest soul. He wondered where Dewey could have gotten to. He would to ask Henry about Dewey. Miss Emily had found the cat outside one morning looking like it would die on the steps. She picked up the poor thing, brought it in, nursed it back to health and named it Dewey. It had been five or six years ago. The cat became a fixture at the library and Buck didn't see any sign of

13

him. This was going to be the most puzzling case of his career and he was sure he wasn't going to like it.

3   BUCK WENT BACK to his office to try to figure things out. Waiting there for him was the editor of the Oak Grove Gazette. Just what he needed a reporter.

"Hey, Buck! What can you tell me on the Emily Meeks murder?" Josh Decker asked anxiously.

"Nothin' yet, Josh. Don't even rightly know it was a murder."

"C'mon, Buck. The whole town is talking about it. Miss Meeks was a legend in this town. A pillar of the community for as long as anyone can remember," Josh argued.

"So, write a story on what her passing will mean for the town. Do something not sensational for a change."

"Like there is ever anything sensational in this town to write about. This could be a big break. News wires might pick up my story. C'mon, Buck, give me something."

"Look, Josh, I don't have anything to give," Buck replied gruffly. "The sweetest lady in town is dead and I have no clue what happened or why. I can't give you what I don't have." He turned and headed into his office.

Josh stood there wondering if it would do any good to follow Buck into the office. Deciding against it, he turned and strolled out the door.

In his office, Buck took out a pad of paper and wrote down Miss Emily Meeks at the top. This is the way he had done it in the city and this is the way he would do it now; none of those big blackboards with photos all over it for him, just a list of the knowns and unknowns. It was how he got things done. He always hated walking into the station and seeing those big blackboards with crime scene photos and the face of the dead. He wouldn't have it here. It was something he'd determined when he'd taken this job. So far, nothing had happened which warranted a huge investigation. A couple of fires, kids drag racing down Old Mill Road, Seth Rankin and his binges, and a couple of silly bar fights at Joe's. This was a quiet town and which is just what he wanted.

>Miss Emily Meeks
>
>Closed library 4:30p.m. Saturday
>
>Where did she go from there?
>
>Did she attend church on Sunday?
>
>Who saw her last?
>
>Did she make any phone calls?
>
>Who is next of kin?
>
>Where is Dewey the cat?
>
>What did she have?
>
>Who ransacked house?
>
>What did they want?
>
>Who ransacked library?
>
>Did they find what they wanted?
>
>How did Miss Emily die?
>
>What made her last moments so horrible?
>
>Who killed her and why??????

Now he had his list, he had a direction to go. Picking up his phone he buzzed his secretary. "Millie, find out who the next of kin is for Miss Emily Meeks. I need to contact them. Also, find out if she made any calls Saturday night or Sunday and who she called." Buck hung up the phone.

Quickly he picked it up again. "Millie, thanks." He was always forgetting to thank people. He was used to just giving orders. His wife kept nagging at him, he was supposed to let people know he appreciated them.

At her desk, Millie smiled and went about the task of locating someone related to Miss Emily as well as tracking down her phone records. Millie had grown up with Buck in Oak Grove. They even dated once or twice in high school. She was a willowy woman with dark hair she kept in a French twist. She had dark eyes and a sallow complexion. Her face was angular giving her a distinct look, though not necessarily a raving beauty, she did turn heads when she entered the room. She had been a clerk at the police station since high school. She'd gone to the junior college in River City to get a secretarial degree and she continued to take classes from time to time to better help her understand law enforcement. She was efficient.

It didn't take Millie long to get the phone records her boss wanted, finding the next of kin was going to be a problem. No one in town knew of any next of kin. Miss Emily had been alone since her parents died twenty years ago. She did remember some story about Miss Emily staying with an aunt to finish out her Master's Degree, but who knew if the aunt was still alive. Millie decided to check the college records where Miss Emily had attended college. They might have something on file.

Buck's phone buzzed shortly after Millie was given her tasks. "Buck here."

"Buck, Doc on line one with the preliminary autopsy report."

"Thanks, Millie." Buck picked up line one. "Ok, Doc, what have we got?"

"Well, I can tell you it was a murder. She was poisoned with something. Tox screen won't be back for a couple of days. Her last moments on earth were horrendous. She was in a lot of pain."

"Ok, Doc, thanks."

"I hope you find the person who did this, Buck. Miss Emily didn't deserve to die this way. She had another twemty years or more in her."

"I want him too, Doc," Buck said sadly. "I don't want this kind of thing in my town."

After hanging up, Buck looked again at his list.

Miss Emily Meeks

Closed library at 4:30 p.m. Saturday.

Where did she go from there?

Did she attend church on Sunday?

Who saw her last?

Did she make any phone calls?

Who is the next of kin?

Where is Dewey the cat?

What did she have?

Who ransacked the house?

What did they want?

Who ransacked the library?

How did Miss Emily die? **MURDER**

What made her last moments so horrible? **POISON**

Who killed her and <u>why?</u>

What kind of poison was it?

After 'How did Miss Emily die?' Buck wrote MURDER. Then after 'What made her last moments so horrible?' he wrote POISON. He underlined the word '<u>why</u>' and added a new question. 'What kind of poison was it?'

He leaned back in his chair and closed his eyes. What did he really know about Emily Meeks?

He'd grown up in this town and Miss Emily had been the librarian all his life. He remembered the first time he'd seen her. He'd been about ten and had to take his little sister to the story time. Miss Emily was dressed in a severe gray dress with her mousy brown hair pulled into a bun. She looked like something out of a storybook. But when she started to read, Buck was hooked. Her voice was like liquid honey. She made the characters jump off the page. He never missed a story time after again.

Miss Emily proved to be a wonderful resource when he hit high school. She helped him find materials for papers he had to do and projects were required. In fact, Miss Emily had helped everyone at some time or other. She was just kind to all who crossed her path. Like the cat, she found on the doorstep.

It had rained hard all night and when she arrived at the library in the morning the poor cat lay rain drenched on the steps. Miss Emily picked it up and took it inside. She made it a warm little bed out of a cardboard box and some old towels. She found an eyedropper somewhere and gave it drops of warm milk until it seemed somewhat revived. Dewey became the unofficial guardian of the library. She even had a contest to find a name for it. Every kid in town was trying to think of a good name. Seems to Buck it was one of the Wilber kids who came up with the name.

Miss Emily had been born to Joe and Mary Meeks when they thought they were too old for a child. Both had been in their late thirties. She had been a quiet and thoughtful child. Her father had died the year before she finished college. She stayed on a year to do her Master's Degree, and then came home to live with her mother. Her mother had died about ten years ago. Emily had been there all through her long illness. She had remained in the house she grew up in.

Who would want to hurt someone like her? Again, Buck looked at his list. This was going to be a puzzle, better get to it and find out where Miss Emily went after leaving the library on Saturday night. It seemed like the logical place to start. He'd call Henry and ask if he noticed which way Miss Emily was going when she left or if she mentioned any plans to him.

A quick call to Henry left Buck even more puzzled. Miss Emily was walking east as Henry recalled. She must have been going somewhere besides home, because her home was to the west of the library. Just as Buck was deciding where to go next, Millie poked her head in the door.

"Buck, I've got some good news and bad news," Millie started.

"C'mon in and let me have it."

"Well, tracing the calls Miss Emily made was easy. There were none."

Buck raised his eyebrows, "Let me guess, that's the good news."

Millie nodded, "The bad news is she didn't stay with an aunt all those years ago. She stayed at a home for unwed mothers."

"Was she working there to help pay for her last year of college?" Buck asked.

"No, it appears she was there because she was having a baby. Although to her credit she did finish her last year of college."

"So, what happened to the baby?" Buck asked.

"It was a girl and she was given up for adoption. Now here's the twist. About three years ago the girl showed up trying to locate her birth mother."

"Do we know who the girl is? Do we know where she is? Did she find her mother?" Buck asked eagerly.

"Not yet, but I've got someone working on it," Millie answered. "And by the way, Josh Decker has called."

"Again? What does he want this time? I'll deal with him tomorrow. When Tom, Jr. gets here with the crime scene photos, lock them in the file. They are going to be pretty bad and I don't want Decker to get a hold of them. Miss Emily should have some dignity. I'm going to see if I can find out where she might have gone after work on Saturday. I'll check in from home tonight."

"Got it, Buck. No one will see those photos, not even me," Millie said. "Don't call from home; I'll leave a message if anything turns up."

"Thanks, Millie."

Buck got up and headed out to find out where Emily Meeks had spent her last hours on earth before going to her home.

4 BUCK HEADED FOR the library. It was a nice day so he walked east and see if he could figure out where Miss Emily was headed. At the library, he found the word was out and people had begun to make a shrine. Flowers, candles, books, photos, posters were lining the steps to the library door, where someone had hung a black wreath. Small towns, Buck thought, where everyone is family.

He turned east to see what he could from the bottom of the steps. The park was on the left side of the road. It was filled with children now school was out. Earlier it would have been filled with the town's senior set, playing shuffleboard, checkers, walking, or talking. Could it have been Miss Emily's destination? Seemed unlikely at 4:30 in the afternoon, especially since she had worked all day. It was something to think about. On the right-hand side of the road, were a few houses and a run-down trailer. Buck started walking, maybe something would come to him or he would see someone who might have seen Miss Emily.

Old Mrs. Wilkes was sitting on her front porch. She'd been cranky even when he was a kid. Buck decided to see if she knew anything. "Evenin', Mrs. Wilkes," Buck said politely as he approached.

"That you, Buck Wise"?" the old woman cackled.

"Yes'um, I was wondering if you saw Miss Emily when she came by her on Saturday evening?"

"Of course, I did. She always comes by for a cup of tea on Saturday," Mrs. Wilkes replied. "Then she stays a while and read to me. Eyes aren't what they used to be."

"I'm sorry to hear, Mrs. Wilkes. Do you remember what time she left?"

"Do I look like the town crier? She always left about six so's she could get home before dark," Mrs. Wilkes spat. "You goin' ta find the person who done this to her?"

"I hope to, Ma'am. You've been a big help. Now I know she came here after the library closed and then went home," Buck replied. "I thank you kindly for your help. Have a good evening," and he turned to leave.

"Just a minute you young whippersnapper!" cried Mrs. Wilkes, "Nobody said Emily Meeks went right home."

"Excuse me," Buck said as he turned back toward the porch.

"Emily left here and was going to the market, then on home," Mrs. Wilkes replied with a satisfied grin.

"Thank you again, Mrs. Wilkes, you've been most helpful," Buck replied. All the while thinking, *Old Battle Axe, wish she told me to begin with.*

This time Buck turned and with a quick stride headed toward Grady's Market. It should be easy to find out what time Miss Meeks left there. Once at Grady's he sought out Bob

Grady. Bob had taken over his father's store a few years back when his father had had enough and retired to Arizona. He found Bob in his office. Bob had put on a few pounds since high school when they both played football. He was round, his face was round, his bald spot was round, and his belly was round. He was also the friendliest man Buck had ever met.

"Hey, Buck, what a nice surprise. Sit down; can I get you some coffee?"

"No, coffee, thanks. But, I will take a seat. I need to talk to you about Saturday evening."

"Sure. What do you need to know?"

"Well, do you remember seeing Miss Meeks come in around 6 o'clock?"

"Can't say I do, but if she was here it'll be on the store video cameras. Hold on and we can check." Bob got up and went into what looked like a closet. He came out holding a videotape and popped it into the TV. When it came on, he fast-forwarded it to around 5:30 p.m.

"I thought if I started it a little earlier we'd have the time for sure."

"Good thinking."

The two men watched the town's folk going about their shopping needs. It was about 6:15 p.m. before Miss Meeks entered the store. She appeared agitated. She was very hesitant going down aisles and kept looking over her shoulder.

"Now that's strange," Bob said. "I've never seen her act so nervous. You think she was being followed?"

"Bob, can I get a copy of the tape? I want to have someone go over every frame and see if we can figure out who or what panicked Miss Emily."

"Sure, Buck, take it with you. Don't think there were any crimes going on Saturday night, but if you find one I know you'll handle it. Good luck. It's a darn shame what happened to Miss Emily. She was a fine lady."

"Thanks, Bob, and you're right, it is a shame."

Buck headed back to the office. He dropped the tape off with his video tech person, make a few more notes and head for home. It'd be about time for dinner when he arrived.

5   BUCK LOOKED AT his list again and made some notes. Things were starting to fill in, although he was also getting more questions. He put the list in his desk and checked the file cabinet for the photos. Millie had put the envelope in the front. It was sealed. Buck would open it later. On the front was a sticky note. It read, 'Josh Decker called three times. Wants to know if you are avoiding him?' Buck swore and tossed the note on his desk.

Miss Emily Meeks

Closed library 4:30 p.m. Saturday.

Where did she go from there? To see Mrs. Wilkes. Left around six o'clock. Arrived Grady's Market 6:15 p.m.

Did she attend church on Sunday?

Who saw her last?

Did she make any phone calls? *NO*

Who is the next of kin? *DAUGHTER*

Where is Dewey the cat?

What did she have?

Who ransacked the house?

What did they want?

Who ransacked the library?

Did they find what they were looking for?

23

How did Miss Emily die? **MURDER**

What made her last moments so horrible?

POISON

Who killed her and <u>why</u>?

What kind of poison was it?

He locked up the office. Waved to the night clerk and headed for home. It had been an awful day. He knew his wife would have questions. The boys might, too.

The boys. They would be a welcome sight tonight. He wondered what they'd been up to all day. They spent a lot of time in the tree house he built a couple of summers ago. He hoped they'd never out grow it.

Joey was ten, all energy and life. His tousled blond hair never stayed in place. He kept everyone on their toes. Jake on the other hand had his mother's red hair. He was the calming influence in the house. He seemed much older than his eight years and they often called him the peacemaker.

He heard the boys upstairs when he walked in. His wife, Ruth, was telling them to wash up for dinner.

"I thought we were waiting for Dad to get home," came the sound of a young voice from above.

"Dad is home," Buck responded.

The bounding of two boys heading for the same place carried through the house with much shouting and cajoling. In a matter of minutes, the boys burst into the kitchen.

"Dad!!!" they shouted in unison.

"Was it really a murder, Dad?" Joey wanted to know.

"Are you going to solve it?" Jake asked.

"Boys, this is not the time or the place for these questions," admonished Ruth.

After dinner Buck and the boys went to the den for some intense video game time. It was then the subject of murder came up again.

"Dad, is it true? Was Miss Meeks murdered?" Joey wanted to know.

"Son, I can't talk about cases I'm working on, but I will tell you it is true. It's a sad thing when someone hurts another person, but Miss Emily was special."

"Tell us about her, Dad," Jake said quietly.

"Well, I remember one time I had to do a paper on the Civil War. I couldn't see the sense in the war. War is just people fighting over something. I didn't see the sense in fighting and killing. Miss Emily had me read a fiction book called, *Across Five Aprils*. It was about two brothers who fought on opposite sides during the war. It made me think differently about this war. I started digging up facts on how the war tore families apart. She had a way of making you look differently at things."

"Thanks, Dad, I'm sure lots of people have stories they could tell about her," Jake replied.

"You know, I think you're right. Why don't you talk to people around town and write down the stories about her? It would make a great book to put in the library in her honor," Buck suggested.

"I'll ask Mrs. Watkins if she will help me," Jake answered. "It might be something I could do for English."

"I'd like to help, too," Joey chimed in.

"Okay, let's go write down Dad's story," Jake said and off they scampered like two dogs after a rabbit.

"You handled her death well, Buck," Ruth said as she entered the room carrying two cups of coffee. "This is going to really rock things in town."

"I know," Buck said sadly. "I wanted to keep this stuff away from the boys. It's why we moved back here from Detroit. I was tired of the senseless killing. Now I have another senseless killing and it's someone I've known most of my life."

"I know you cannot discuss it, but do you have any clues?"

"Not a one. Which is what doesn't make sense. Miss Emily wouldn't hurt anyone. If someone wanted to rob her, she would have just given them what they asked for and probably served them dinner. She didn't have to die."

Ruth put down her coffee and went to rub Buck's shoulders. "I know this is hard on you. Just try to let it go for tonight. You'll have a better outlook in the morning."

"You're probably right." Buck leaned into her soothing hands and closed his eyes. Ruth, the love of

his life, still as beautiful as the day he met her. She was tall about five feet eight inches. He liked to looking into her green eyes. They seemed to sparkle just like she did. She had the most beautiful red hair. It was a golden fire crowning her slender face and fell below her shoulders. She hardly looked like she had two children.

6 BUCK ARRIVED EARLY at the office Tuesday morning. He was hoping there would be some word from the tech department on the Grady Market video. Clues in this case were scarce. Instead he found Josh Decker waiting for him.

"Good Morning, Chief."

"Hello, Josh. What brings you out so early?"

"I want to know what's going on in the Meeks murder."

"I told you yesterday when I had something, I'd let you know. I don't have anything ready for the press. Now if you'll excuse me, I have a town to protect."

Josh stood outside the door to the station and wondered what Buck was trying to hide from him. *What did Buck know?*

Buck thought of Josh as an oily worm. He arrived in town about five years ago. Took over the Oak Grove Gazette and tried to make it into a gossip rag. He had done nothing over the years, to change the image. His dark hair, dark eyes, and thin body just gave him a look which said shady to Buck.

Millie arrived about an hour later. She knocked on Buck's open door.

"C'mon in, Millie."

"Mornin', Buck."

"Morning. How are we coming on locating the daughter?"

"Well, it seems she lives about twenty miles away in River City. She has a couple of kids. Her name is Ella Mitchell."

"Get me her phone number; I want to call before I go over there. Make sure I have directions, too, and we better let Mike Adams know I'm going to be visiting his town."

"Sure thing, Buck," Millie retreated to her desk to take care of those things and to see if anything new had come in during the night shift.

The phone on Buck's desk rang, "Buck here."

"Sheriff Adams on line one, Buck."

"Thanks, Millie," Buck replied. "Hey, Mike!" he said into the phone.

"Hear you're coming into town today, Buck. Need some help on an apprehension?"

"No, Mike. This one is a condolence call. You know an Ella Mitchell?"

"Yeah, Ella is the daughter-in-law of the Mayor, married to his son, Matt. Who would she know in Oak Grove?" Mike asked puzzled.

"Seems Miss Emily Meeks was her birth mother," Buck replied.

"Miss Emily the librarian?" an astonished Mike asked.

"One and the same."

"She died? I didn't know. Boy, she kept this secret to keep all these years."

"Sure was. Mike, keep this close to you, Miss Emily was murdered." Buck said.

"Well, I'll be. You stop by here before you leave and we'll talk," Mike said.

"I was planning to. See you this afternoon."

Buck pulled together all his notes and started out of the office on his way to River City. As he left, he said, "Millie, I'll be in River City and you can reach me on my radio or cell phone."

Just then Rick Brinks the president of the Oak Grove Bank came barging in.

"Buck, you're just the man I want to see," he said breathlessly.

"Can it wait Rick? I'm just on my way to River City."

"No, this has to do with Miss Meeks.

Seeing the banker was agitated, Buck led him to his office and closed the door.

"Sit down, Rick, and tell me what this is all about," Buck said calmly.

The banker paced a few minutes then sat on the edge of the chair. "I...I just don't know where to start."

"Slowly, start slowly at the beginning."

"Well, when I heard about what happened to Miss Meeks yesterday, I followed procedure and froze her accounts."

"Go on."

"I also learned she had a safe deposit box. So, I froze it, too. Didn't want someone to just think they could come in and empty it. Although I sure don't know who would be coming in," he rambled.

Buck got up and poured two cups of coffee. He put cream in the one he handed to the banker.

"So, you followed procedure and froze the accounts. What does it have to do with me?"

"Well, you see, Buck," he began, "when someone dies, we freeze the accounts until we have proof of the next of kin. We also run a statement to see when the last activity was on any accounts held and how much is in each one."

"I'm with you so far, Rick."

"It's like this," he paused, "we never thought much about it until we got the print outs."

"Are you telling me someone else has been using the account?" Buck asked.

"No."

"What is it then that has you in a tizzy this morning?"

"It's the amount in the accounts." Rick slurped a drink of coffee. "I…well, I …"

"Slow down. What is it?"

"Miss Meeks has millions of dollars in her accounts. I cannot think where she got all the money. I mean she was just the librarian," he sputtered.

Buck said nothing for a minute. Then he asked, "Rick, did you bring a copy of those print outs?"

"Well, no. But I can run back and get them for you," he offered.

"Not necessary. I'll have Millie walk back with you and you can give her a copy. I have some business I need to get to in River City. I want to thank you for bringing this to my attention." Buck calmly led Brinks to the door. He briefly told Millie to escort Brinks to the bank and get copies of the print outs on Miss Emily's account. Then he headed for his car and River City.

7 THE DRIVE TO River City was short. Finding the home of Ella Mitchell wasn't as hard as he thought it was going to be.

The house was a brick ranch in an L shape on a street of houses lined with ranch homes and paved drives. This one set back farther from the road and had a well-maintained lawn. Buck had called ahead to say he was coming. Ella Mitchell told him the kids were gone for the day to come on over.

Buck rang the doorbell. He was shocked when Ella Mitchell answered the door. She was the spitting image of Miss Emily when he was a boy.

"Uh… Mrs. Mitchell?"

"I'm Ella Mitchell, you must be Chief Wise. Won't you come in?"

She had the warm honey voice he remembered from childhood. It was disconcerting to him considering what he had to say.

"I hope you won't mind talking in the kitchen. I have some pies to finish baking. I've made some coffee."

"It's fine," was all Buck could manage as he followed her down the hall to the kitchen.

The house was neat and the walls were light in color. It gave it an airy feeling. The kitchen smelled of apple pie. Buck took a seat on a stool at the bar. Ella busied herself getting two cups of coffee.

"Do you want milk or sugar in your coffee, Chief Wise?"

"No, Ma'm, and please call me Buck."

She turned and handed him a cup of steaming black coffee. "What was it you wanted to see me about?"

"This might be better if you were sitting down he said."

She pulled out a stool on her side of the counter and sat.

"First, I need to ask you a couple of questions."

"Ok."

"I understand Miss Emily Meeks was your birth mother."

"Yes, she is."

"Have you met her?"

"We met about three years ago. She comes here once a month on Sunday for dinner and to visit with her grandchildren. Why has something happened to her?"

"I'm afraid so, Mrs. Mitchell."

"What? Where is she? I need to go to her," Ella frantically cried.

Buck came around the counter and put his hands on her shoulders to keep her seated. She looked up at him with those same grey eyes he knew so well.

"Miss Meeks was killed sometime over the weekend," Buck said calmly.

Ella gasped. Tears formed in her eyes. Her voice quavered as she said, "Tell me how."

"I can't tell you everything and I will need to ask you some questions. As far as we can tell she was poisoned sometime after she got home Saturday night."

Seeing Mrs. Mitchell did not move, Buck slowly lowered his hands. He took a step back and waited. The tears he saw form in her eyes spilled quietly down her cheeks.

Finally, she said, "I'll need to make some arrangements. Can you help me?"

"I can," said Buck. "Are you up to a few more questions?"

She took a sip of her coffee and nodded. Buck went back to his stool and sat down. He pulled a small notebook from his pocket along with his pen. After a moment, he began, "When was the last time you talked to Miss Emily?"

She gave a nervous giggle. "She said people called her Miss Emily. I spoke with her on Friday. She was coming here next week-end."

"Did she seem nervous about anything?"

"Not that I recall."

"Had she mentioned being threatened or followed?"

"No. She was excited about coming. We just chatted about the kids and what I was doing. Nothing seemed any different than usual."

"Were you aware your mother, uh hem, Miss Meeks had substantial sums of money?"

"Em and I did not discuss her finances," Ella said sharply. "What do you mean by substantial?"

"I'm not sure yet, but I believe it to be in the millions," Buck said and watched for a reaction.

"Millions!" Ella choked, "it's not possible. Em was just a town librarian. She didn't make the kind of money it takes to amass millions. There must be some mistake."

"I'll know more when I get back and see the bank records," Buck said. "Do you have any idea about her will?"

"I know she wrote one after we met," Ella replied, "but I don't know the contents. She had a lawyer…Ben something."

"Do you know of anything she had someone might want to steal?" he continued.

"If you know her, you've seen her house. It was all she had as far as I know."

"I want to thank you, Mrs. Mitchell, for your time. If you think of anything else, you can call me at the office. Here is my card. Check with me in a couple of days and I'll have the papers so we can release her body." Buck handed her his card and stood to go. "Oh, by the way, do you have a key to her safety deposit box?"

"No, why would I? I didn't even know she had a safety deposit box." Ella said.

"Well, I'm going to get a court order to open it. If there is anything of value, I will see you get it when the investigation is over."

Buck made his way to the front door with Ella behind him. He again thanked her and headed for his car. It was time to stop by and see Mike Adams.

Ella stood for a few minutes in the doorway watching Buck drive away. When she closed the door she leaned against it and sobbed uncontrollably. Her mother, whom she'd only just begun to know, had been murdered. Why? What other secrets did she have? What was she hiding besides me? Where did she get millions?

8 BUCK DROVE QUICKLY to the Sheriff's office. He was ushered into the office as soon as he arrived. Mike Adams' secretary returned with two cups of coffee and the two men settled down to talk.

"Ok, Buck, tell me about Miss Emily. How did she die?"

"Well, Doc Reed says she was poisoned. Also says her last few moments were very painful."

"Has he said what kind of poison?"

"Tox won't be back before tomorrow."

"Boy, this is hard to grasp. Miss Emily was an institution in Oak Grove.Why I remember the time she caught Betty Jean Johnson and I necking in the listening room. She gave us quite the lecture," Mike chuckled at the thought.

"You be sure and tell my boys the story. They are collecting stories about Miss Emily to put in a book."

"Cute idea, so what did you learn from Ella Mitchell?"

"Have you ever seen her?"

"Nope can't say's I have. Why?"

"She looks like Miss Emily when we were kids. Sure, took me back in time to see her."

"She a suspect?"

"Nope, just the next of kin. She was pretty broken up when I told her, tried hard not to let it show."

"Well, I need to get back to the office and make some notes. Also got to look at some bank statements. Old Rick Brinks was huffin' and puffin' about Miss Emily having millions. Can you imagine?"

Mike chuckled. "Now it would be something. See ya 'round, Buck."

Buck nodded and made his way to the door. As he started out, he turned to his old friend and said, "Don't be a stranger. Ruth and the boys would love for you to come to dinner."

Mike waved and looked at the papers on his desk. Buck headed for his car. Once in the car he radioed Millie to let her know he was on his way back.

9 THE OFFICE WAS in an uproar when he got back. Josh Decker was leading the parade. As soon as he saw Buck he made a bee line for him.

"Is it true Chief? Did Miss Meeks have a secret fortune? Was she killed for her money? What took you out of town today? Did it have to do with the Meeks' murder?" he fired his questions rapidly without waiting for a response.

"I don't know where you find this stuff, Josh. You should be ashamed of yourself for getting' these good people worked up over nothin'," Buck replied calmly. Turning to the crowd he said, "Those of you with police complaints form a line at the counter and Millie will take your name and complaint. The rest of you go on home. This is no place to be hanging around."

There were many moans and groans, but in no time the mass of people in the office dwindled to Millie, Buck and Josh.

"Much better,' Buck stated. "Millie, if there's anything new I'll be in my office."

"C'mon, Buck, it's an old trick. You need to make a statement. You *are* the officer in charge," complained Josh.

"Ok," Buck said with resignation. "Here's my statement: The death of Miss Emily Meeks is a tragedy and we are looking into it. When we have something to report, I will issue a full statement." He turned on his heal and went into his office closing the door.

Josh looked at the empty room, said, "Well!" and strolled out.

Inside Buck's office Millie was showing him the print outs from the bank.

"I would never have guessed this," Buck said.

"Me, either. I thought she was just getting by. Look at the way her house was run down."

"The daughter didn't seem to know about it either."

"What's she like?" questioned Millie.

"Do you remember what Miss Emily looked like when we were kids? Mousy brown hair, huge gray eyes, slender figure, full hips, this girl could be her twin."

"Wow! Really she could?"

"Yep, and her voice has the same warm honey sound Miss Emily's had. I think she was really trying to get to know Miss Emily."

"Poor kid, bet she's going to take this hard," Millie mused.

"I think the grandkids are the ones it will really hurt," said Buck. "Didn't see them so, don't know how many there are, but she was supposed to be going there next Sunday for dinner."

Millie was quiet. Then she said, "There has to be something else we don't know."

"I'm sure there is. Miss Emily was full of secrets."

"What an understatement." Millie headed for her desk leaving Buck to sort out the bank printouts.

Just as the door closed, Buck said, "Ella Mitchell might call. I told her we'd have the papers in a few days for her to sign to release the body."

Millie nodded and closed his door.

10

BUCK REACHED FOR his pad. It was time to make some additions to the list. He sure didn't feel like he was making progress.

Miss Emily Meeks

Closed library 4:30 p.m. Saturday.

Where did she go from there? To see Mrs. Wilkes. Left around 6 o'clock. Arrived Grady's Market 6:15 p.m.

Did she attend church on Sunday?

Who saw her last?

Did she make any phone calls? NO

Who is the next of kin? DAUGHTER, Ella Mitchell, River City, seems broken up

Where is Dewey the cat?

What did she have? Could it have been $

Who ransacked the house?

What did they want?

Who ransacked the library?

Did they find what they were looking for?

How did Miss Emily die? **MURDER**

What made her last moments so horrible? **POISON**

Who killed her and <u>why</u>?

What kind of poison was it?

Where did the money come from?

What's in the safe deposit box?

Are there any other secrets?

Why does Josh Decker keep turning up?

Buck felt like he was getting more questions than answers. He'd chase down Rick Brinks at the bank tomorrow and see if Rick could tell him when the transactions were made and how often. It might give him a clue as to where the money came from. He also needed to track down the person who drew up Miss Emily's will. There might be a clue or two there, too. Maybe Ben Wallace was the attorney who did. Buck made a note to call Ben in the morning. He also needed to check with Doc Reed on the final autopsy and the toxin screen. Tomorrow would be a very busy day.

Buck put away the Emily Meeks file and began going through his in box for anything which had to be taken care of before he left for home. Finding nothing, he headed for home.

Buck found his family in the backyard setting the table for a cookout. He didn't remember they were planning to entertain, but before he could ask the doorbell rang. To his surprise, he found himself face to face with Mike Adams.

"Hi, Buck. Thought I'd take you up on your offer to visit the family. Brought Betsy Tate with me, hope you don't mind," he said cheerfully.

"Nope, not a problem, hi, Betsy."

"Hi, Buck, long time no see," she replied as she leaned in to give him a hug.

"Ruth and the boys are in the back, just give me a minute to change and I'll join you."

Mike and Betsy made their way through the house to the backyard.

"Uncle Mike!" the boys shouted as they charged at him.

Betsy made her way to Ruth and asked, "Is there anything I can help with?"

"No, I've got everything under control. As soon as Buck gets here, he'll take over at the grill and you and I can go to the kitchen and finish up there."

"Sounds great."

Buck stood in the back door for a minute just taking in the scene of his childhood friend rolling in the grass with his sons and his wife talking to Mike's long-time girlfriend. *He should just marry the girl,* Buck thought.

Seeing Buck, Ruth waved the spatula. It was his cue to join the merriment and make the hamburgers. He walked over to his wife, gave her a kiss on the cheek and said, "I see you have everything well underway."

"Yep, I thought we should take advantage of the nice weather. When Mike called, I told him we were going to have a picnic and to bring Betsy. I hope you don't mind."

"Nope, it's a great idea. I wanted to bounce a couple of things off Mike anyway."

"No shop-talk! This is a picnic, it's family time," Ruth admonished.

The evening was nice. The boys had a good time. After they went up to bed, Buck suggested he and Mike check out the tree house. Being boys at heart the two men climbed the ladder leadinig to the little house in the tree.

"I'm impressed, built in beds. We never had it this good," Mike commented.

"I know. I went a bit overboard. I wanted it to be the perfect place for the boys."

"Well, it is. Now what's up we had to climb a tree?"

"It's the Emily Meeks thing. Mike, she could have owned the whole town and still had money left over. Where did a small-town librarian get that kind of money? Is it what she was killed for?"

Mike thought for a moment. "Did she get some kind of life insurance or inheritance from her parents? Did she make some smart investments?"

"I don't know. The more I try to find answers, the more questions I get. I thought I knew Miss Emily, but it seems she had quite a few secrets," replied Buck.

"Use that methodical brain of yours, start with a list of the secrets and see where they lead you?"

"Thanks, Mike. And while we're here I thought you might like one of these." Buck reached into his shirt and brought out two cold cans of beer. He handed one to Mike.

After Mike and Betsy left, Buck commented to Ruth, "Mike should just marry Betsy. He could use a couple of kids of his own."

"He could," his wife agreed. "I think Betsy is more than ready to be his wife."

"Ah, well, Mike always was a bit slow. Guess I better call him in the morning and put a bug in his ear." With a chuckle, he kissed his wife and turned out the light.

11

BUCK HAD A list of things to do when he got to work on Wednesday. He told Millie to get Doc Reed, Ben Wallace, and Rick Brinks on the phone. He didn't care what order, but he needed to talk to all of them. He also told her to light a fire under the tech department; he needed some answers about the video.

"Will do, Buck, and by the way, Josh Decker has already called this morning," Millie said.

"What in tarnation does he want now?" Buck asked irritably.

"Said you were holding back on the Meeks case and he wanted some answers."

"What is his interest in all this? There have been suspicious things in the past and he didn't care." Buck commented. "I want you to do a background check on him, too, Millie. He hasn't been around here more than five years. He always wants something sensational, but he's never been this aggressive in the past."

"I'll get on it as soon as I make your calls."

"Thanks, Millie."

The first call to get through was Doc Reed. "Buck, I was waiting for you to call. I have the final autopsy report and the tox screen."

"Ok, Doc, give me what you have."

"Emily Meeks died of respiratory failure due to poisoning. The poison used was gelsemium."

"What is gelsemium and where does it come from, Doc?"

"It comes from the Yellow Jasmine. You know those big yellow flowers Miss Emily kept in her kitchen? The ones she kept in her miniature hothouse."

"What did she do, eat one?"

"No, the poison comes from the root. Someone boiled it into her tea. Sad thing is it paralyzes the system. It starts working immediately, but can take up to half an hour before it's actually set in. Then death comes anywhere from one to seven and a half hours later. She was conscious through most of it. She knew she was going to die."

"So, do we have a time of death? Why on earth would someone want to drag out her death?"

"Time of death is an approximation. Killer probably left long before she was gone. I show it to be about 4:00 to 4:30 a.m. on Sunday. Looks like it was ingested some time between 8:30 and 9:00 p.m. the night before."

"So, you think the killer left before then?"

"Sure, you want to hang around when someone's bladder lets go? Once she was under the influence of the poison, there was no reason to stay. Not sure if the killer knew how long it would take her to die."

"Thanks, Doc. Send Millie the report."

Buck hung up the phone. Miss Emily was killed by her own plant. It had to be of some significance. He wondered where she got the plant. It sure wasn't native to this area. And to think she was conscious most of the time. He wished it had been quick for her.

Buck picked up his phone, "Millie, have we heard anything from the tech department? I want to know what is on the tape."

"Andy Hall is right here, Buck. I had him wait until you were off the phone."

"Send him in now!" Buck put down the phone and headed toward his TV to get it ready.

Andy Hall entered the room and closed the door. "Sorry, it took so long, Buck. I wanted to be sure of what I was seeing."

"Well, let's both see it now and you can tell me what you found suspicious."

The video came on the screen. Andy began his narration. "You see MissMeeks for the first time a 6:15 p.m. She appears nervous and agitated and keeps looking over her shoulder. Now watch this."

Josh Decker appears on the screen in front of Miss Emily. She drops the can she is holding. He talks to her for a minute, retrieves the can, hands it to her, and walks on down the aisle. Miss Emily proceeds to the check out where she fumbles her money. Then she almost races to the taxi stand.

"Strange," Buck said, "Miss Emily never takes a cab."

"What I thought. And the time is clearly 6: 35 p.m."

"Thanks, Andy. I'll get a hold of Butch at the taxi stand and see if she went right home."

Andy got up to leave. Just before he opened the door he turned to ask Buck, "Do you think Josh Decker had anything to do with this?"

"At this point, Andy, I don't think anything."

Andy closed the door on his way out.

Buck was getting more confused. Millie buzzed to say she had Rick Brinks on line one.

"Rick, I need to know if you can tell me how Miss Emily made her deposits. Did she deposit checks, were they at ATM's, or were they regular? Just how did she come by this money?"

The banker hesitated the said, "I'm not sure if is information I can give out, Buck."

"Rick, this is a murder investigation. Miss Emily is not here to complain," Buck sternly replied. "Get me the information or I'm going to appear in your bank at the busiest time with a court order and I'm going to make as much of a ruckus as I can."

The banker hemmed and hawed, but finally relented, "I'll get it over to you right away. No need for you to come in here, Buck."

"I thought you'd see it my way," Buck said as he hung up the phone. When he was done he looked up to see Ben Wallace standing in his doorway.

"You going to try to strong arm me, too, Buck?" he asked.

"Can't see where I'd need to, Ben," was Buck's reply. "I just need to know a couple of things from you. They shouldn't even come closed to breaking confidentiality."

Ben came in closed the door and took a seat in front of Buck's desk. He was dressed in an old brown, corduroy suit with suede patches at the elbows. He was a man of about sixty with white hair and a slight paunch. Once he settled himself he looked at Buck.

"What is it you think I might know?"

"Well, Ben, I need to know if Miss Meeks had you write up her will."

"She did."

"How long ago?" Buck asked.

"'Bout three years."

"So, can you tell me who gets what?" a frustrated Buck asked.

"Nope. You can be at the reading. I won't know when it is until I've talked with the next of kin."

"The next of kin, be Ella Mitchell?"

"Yes."

"Did you know how big her estate was?"

"What do you mean big? She had her old house and a few bucks in the bank," Ben sputtered.

"Well, the few bucks in the bank amounts to over five million dollars," Buck announced.

"Five million!!!!" Ben shouted. "Where in the world did Emily get that kind of money?"

"I can see you're as stunned as the rest of us," replied Buck with a grin. "I've got Rick Brinks over at the bank lookin' into it right now. It's the strong arm you heard when you came in."

"Well, I'll be," mused Ben, "Who'd a thought Emily could be a millionaire? Miss Ella's going to be in for quite a surprise."

"I'm afraid it won't be too much of a surprise, Ben. I was over there yesterday. She was shocked at the thought her mother had millions."

"I'll bet she was. Poor kid has been through a lot in her life."

"What makes you say so, Ben? She's married to the mayor's son. She's got a lovely home."

Well, Buck, it's like this; Emily gave her child up for adoption thirty years ago. Couple who took her was young. Both only children, their parents were dead. They'd grown up in an orphanage and didn't want it to happen to another child. Ella was the first of two children they adopted. When the boy was about six there was a car accident. Ella and the boy were sent to foster care. He was adopted right off, but Ella went from home to home. She figured out early her smarts were her ticket to a better life. Graduated top of her class and got a scholarship to college. Studied accounting and passed her CPA exam the first time. Got hired by some fancy accounting firm in the college town and started working on her Master's Degree. It's when she met Matt Mitchell. His parents were opposed to the marriage. They've come around but sure made those first few years hard for the kids."

"So how did she come to find Miss Emily?"

"She got interested in genealogy when she was home with her first baby and ended up coming here to get Emily to help her about six years ago. Imagine her surprise when she and Emily met."

"I'll bet Miss Emily got a shock, too," Buck mused.

"Sure did. Called me the same afternoon and I had dinner with her the same night. She was fit to by tied. I talked her into getting to know the girl. Three weeks later she called about changing her will."

"How many kids does she have?"

"Well as I recall, there are three. The little girl, Jane Emily, is the oldest and the twins are next, boy and a girl, Tyler Matthew and Emily Ella."

"They were just getting to know their grandmother. Now, this," Buck said sadly. "Thanks for your help, Ben. Let me know when the will reading is."

"Will do," Ben said as he got to his feet. "Make sure this guy pays will you, Buck."

"I will, Ben. I will."

The two men shook hands and Ben Wallace left the office. Buck found himself a cup of coffee and sat down at the desk. He needed to make some more notes. He took out his pad and looked over what he had already written. To the list, he would add what he had learned from Doc Reed, Ben Wallace, and Andy Hall. Did he have the whole picture yet? Somehow, he doubted it. The information coming from the bank might be the link he needed to put it all together.

Just then Millie came in. She was holding some documents looking like a rap sheet.

"This just came in, Buck, and I knew you'd want it right away."

"What is it, Millie?"

"Background check on Josh Decker; aka Jason Decks, and Joe Dee. Seems our little Josh gets around. Mostly petty stuff, but he did do a couple years for trying to swindle an elderly lady out of her money."

"Well, this sure puts a new twist on things. Seems everybody has some secrets in this town," Buck commented thoughtfully.

"Are you going to want to talk to him?" Millie inquired.

"Not just yet, but this does put him on the suspect list. Thanks for the update, Millie," Buck said. He took the papers she handed him to add to the notes he needed to add to his sheet. "I'll be heading home shortly. Need to take a run by the library first."

"Won't be able to get up the steps. People been leaving things there for three days now."

"Thanks, Millie."

Again, Buck looked at his notes.

Miss Emily Meeks

Closed library 4:30 p.m. Saturday.

Where did she go from there? To see Mrs. Wilkes. Left around 6 o'clock. Arrived Grady's Market 6:15 p.m.

Did she attend church on Sunday? No

Who saw her last? Taxi driver??

Did she make any phone calls? NO

Who is the next of kin? DAUGHTER, Ella Mitchell, River City, seems broken up

Where is Dewey the cat?

What did she have? *Could it have been $*

Who ransacked the house?

What did they want?

Who ransacked the library?

Did they find what they were looking for?

How did Miss Emily die? **MURDER**

What made her last moments so horrible? **POISON**—conscious, knew she was dying

Who killed her and why? *Was it for the money?*

What kind of poison was it? *Gelsemium* from plant root, paralytic, painful death

Where did the money come from?

What's in the safe deposit box?

Secrets? Miss Emily has daughter, Miss Emily had millions. Josh Decker has criminal record.

Why does Josh Decker keep turning up? Has a criminal background. Was seen talking to Miss Emily in grocery store.

Who is in the will?

Buck finished his notes. He put everything in the file, put it in the file cabinet and locked it. He then left and walked toward the library.

He found out Millie was right. There was no way to get to the front door. Every space on every step had a memento of some kind. Children made drawings, others left flowers, and candles. This had become a shrine. He hoped Josh Decker had taken photos of this for his newspaper. It might make a good story.

12 **BUCK HAD BEEN** putting off going into the library. Now he took Millie and two others in to begin going through the mess. He had arranged with the high school to have some of the kids come and put the books back on the shelves. Miss Emily had sponsored a group of young people who took turns working in the library. They would know how to put things back together.

47

Today's mission was to see if one of the many papers scattered all over was a clue. Millie came along because all papers were going to be given to her. She would bag them and tag them as evidence. Once the papers were back at the station, they would be gone through them and see if there were any usable fingerprints. Then the contents would be examined to see if there was any useful information.

They had been at it about three hours when the phone rang. Everyone stopped for a minute. Then in her usual efficient way, Millie answered it.

"Oak Grove Library, how may I help you?"

There was silence on the other end.

"May I help you?" Millie asked again. The line went dead.

"Now that was strange. Do we need to put a tap on this line?"

Buck quickly replied, "No, I'm not putting someone in here twenty-four hours a day to see if the person calls again. It might just have been someone who wondered where Miss Emily was."

"Well they could have asked," Millie said, "I'd have told them."

"We'll be done here in a couple of hours anyway. The boys have stacked as many books as they can. The kids from the high school will be in tomorrow to get them back on the shelf. Then Henry Watson, can get back to work," said Buck.

They were locking up when Ella Mitchell showed up. She had dark circles under her eyes. Millie looked shocked when she saw her.

"Mrs. Mitchell, what are you doing here?" asked

"I came to sign the papers so they would release Em's body. The girl at the desk told me you were here."

"I'm sorry you had to come here."

"It's not a problem. It was nice to see the wonderful tribute paid to her outside."

Millie piped in, "Why don't you walk back to the office with me? I know where the papers are and I'll help you get things taken care of."

"It's very kind of you."

"No problem. Buck, I'll see you back at the office."

Buck nodded and got everyone back to work loading things into the cars to take back to the office. It had been a long day and there was still more to do.

Back at the office, Millie got Ella a cup of coffee and set her in a conference room. She then went to her desk and got the papers Ella would need to sign. She told Betty Sue she'd deal with her later. Betty Sue just shrugged her shoulders and went back to filing her nails.

"Let me apologize again, Mrs. Mitchell," she said as she entered the room. "I thought I'd set these papers out in case you came in."

"It's no problem."

"I'm sorry, I was a bit taken a back at the library. You look so much like Miss Emily did when I was growing up."

"Yes, it was quite a shock when I first met her. It was like seeing what I will look like when I grow older. Although fifty-two isn't what I'd call old."

"No is sure isn't," agreed Millie. "I'm surprised I didn't see you around town."

"After our first meeting, I didn't come to Oak Grove. We agreed it would be better if she came to see me," Ella explained. "You know how people in small towns gossip. Em kept me a secret all these years. I didn't want people to think any less of her."

"You mean she didn't want to shout from the library steps she was a grandmother?"

"No, I don't think it bothered her at all. I think she had an image she needed to protect." Ella paused for a minute then continued. "You were her people, her town, and she had watched many of you grow upYou were the family she didn't want to disappoint."

"I see what you mean." Millie showed Ella where to sign and gave her the copy to take with her to the funeral home. "Have you met Josh Decker yet?"

"No, I've only met you and Chief Wise. Why do you ask?"

"Josh Decker took over the Oak Grove Gazette about five years ago. He changed it from a small town paper to a scandal rag. He's been nosing around here for information about Miss Emily's death."

"Oh, I have nothing to say to the press at this time," Ella said earnestly. "I'm not ready to divulge family secrets or anything."

"Ok, then let's do this." Millie sketched out a plan to call the funeral home, talk to Will Williams and have him come pick up the papers. Then Ella wouldn't chance a meeting with Josh Decker until the funeral. He was sure to show up then. Ella agreed to the plan. After it was taken care of and she gave her requirements to the funeral director, Millie led her to her car, checking first to see Josh was not lurking around.

13 THE FUNERAL WAS set for 11 am on Saturday, because the turn out was expected to be high, the funeral would be held in the high school gym. The casket would be closed and photos of Emily Meeks would be displayed at each end of the coffin. One end would have photos of her childhood and the

other would have more recent photos, including some with her daughter and grandchildren.

People started arriving at 9:30 a.m. They walked by the casket, took time to look at the photos, some laid flowers on the casket. There were so many flowers it was hard to place them all.

Ella Mitchell, her husband, Matt, and the three children sat in the front row. Many of the towns' people were shocked to know Miss Emily had a grown daughter and grandchildren, still remembered their manners and stopped to say a few kind words to the family.

Ella was overwhelmed by the amount of people and the kind words they had to say. Matt reached over to hold her hand. He knew how hard this was for her. It was then the trouble started.

Josh Decker had come up an outside aisle with his camera. He started snapping pictures of the people at the casket and those who stopped to say a few kind words to Ella Mitchell. Ella didn't notice until Tyler tugged on her jacket. She looked to where her pointed just in time for the flash to go off in her face. She was appalled to think someone would be taking pictures at a funeral.

Matthew sensing her displeasure arose and walked toward the man with the camera. "Excuse me, what are you doing here?"

"I own the local paper and I'm getting pictures."

"I don't think so," replied Matt angrily. "This is a funeral not a wedding. Take your camera and leave."

"It's a public place and I have a right to be here."

"It may be a public place, but you have no right to be here. You are not paying respects. Kindly leave or I will escort you out."

By this time, a crowd was gathering around the two men. Josh could sense the hostility around him.

"I'm covered by the first Amendment."

"Well, let the first Amendment cover you outside," Matt replied. He reached to take Josh by the arm and escort him from the room.

"I'll take it from here," Buck said with authority. "Come on, Josh, you've caused enough trouble for one day."

"But I have a right..."

Ben Wallace said angrily, "A right to what, disrupt the funeral of a decent woman and harass her family? I don't think so, young man."

Seeing he was out numbered, Josh reluctantly allowed Buck to lead him out of the gym. Once outside, Buck asked one of his deputies to keep him out of the school.

"If he gives you any trouble, lock him in the jail." Turning, Buck returned to the gym. He made his way to the front, offered apologies to Ella and Matt Mitchell and took his seat with his family.

Reverend Parker, the Methodist minister had agreed to do the ceremony. He kept if very short and focused on the good Emily Meeks had done over the years for the town and the people in it. Prayers were said and the Reverend asked for donations be made to the library in the form of books or cash. Dinner would be after burial at the Knights of Columbus Hall and all were welcome to come and share their memories with Miss Emily's daughter and her family.

Many of the towns' people came to the hall to speak to Miss Emily's daughter. The ladies wanted to get a look at this girl they had never known about. This would feed the town gossips for months to come. They all wanted to see the grandchildren.

SECRETS

Ella was not prepared for the kindness of the people of Oak Grove. There was enough food to feed an army. Both the Oak Grove Cafe and the diner donated time and people to put together a spread which would feed the town. Food was set up all around the outsides of the hall, with lines able to go on each side of the table. There was chicken, turkey, ham, even hamburgers and hot dogs for the kids. Every imaginable salad had been made. There were mashed potatoes, sweet potatoes, someone even made scalloped potatoes. The dessert table was also laden with everything from Jell-O to brownies, cookies, pies, and several kinds of cakes. No one would go hungry this day.

It didn't take long for Ella's three children to find other children who would keep them busy and tell them about their grandmother. She also found many people who wanted to tell her stories.

The biggest surprise came from Joey and Jake Wise.

"Excuse us, Mrs. Mitchell?"

"Yes?"

"I'm Joey Wise and this is my brother, Jake. We've been talking to people in town about Miss Meeks."

"Go on."

"Well, we thought it would be nice to have all the stories about her in a book, but we couldn't write fast enough. So, Dad got us a tape recorder and we got people to tell us about her on tape. We wanted you to have it," he said quietly as he handed her a shoebox full of cassette tapes.

Ella couldn't contain the tears from running down her face at the boys' thoughtfulness. "Thank you both. This is the nicest thing you could have done for me."

The boys stood there awkwardly before running off to join their friends.

The day couldn't have ended soon enough for Ella. People had been more than kind. She had been given enough food for a week. Her emotions were shattered and she was beyond tired. After putting the kids to bed, she curled up in her favorite chair and held the box of tapes.

Matt came in carrying a glass of wine and asked, "Do you want to listen to them now?"

"No, I think I'll wait. It was just the kindest thing to do. I want to save them for the kids. Right now, I just want to sit. I feel numb."

Matt took the box from her and set it on the coffee table. He pulled her into his arms and just held her. Ella stayed in the safety of his arms and just cried.

14 BUCK SPENT HIS Sunday with his family. He and the boys did lawn work, while Ruth did what he called woman's work. At noon, he decided it was time they take a break.

"What do you say we take a picnic lunch and go down to the creek? We might even try some fishing."

To a chorus of, "Yeah!" Ruth entered the backyard.

"What's all the yelling about?" she asked.

"Dad says we can go to the creek," Joey said excitedly.

"And fishing," Jake chimed in.

"Oh, did he now?" she asked with a chuckle. "Who do you suppose is going to fix lunch?"

Very seriously Jake said, "You, Mom. We're going to have a picnic."

Everyone laughed and Ruth said, "Well, it just so happens there is a picnic basket on the kitchen table just waiting for a place to go."

The boys dashed toward the house with Buck and Ruth bringing up the rear. They loaded the car and took off for a secluded stretch of beach Buck knew from his childhood. Once there the boys waded into the water to do some fishing, which turned out to be some splashing.

Ruth and Buck spread a blanket and set back to enjoy the afternoon. It wasn't long before Buck said, "Nice turn out for Miss Emily yesterday."

"Yes, it was. Too, bad Josh Decker had to barge in."

"Yes, he sure upset everyone. Wonder if he really thinks someone will buy funeral photos."

"I sure won't," said Ruth angrily. Then, "I think Ella Mitchell is a fine young woman."

"I think you're right. I'm going to have to call her tomorrow and tell her, she can have the key to the house. It's hers now. We have gone over it."

"Let her know, if she needs someone to be with her, I'm available."

"I will," Buck said. "I'd rather you help her than some of the busy bodies in town."

They had lunch and watched the boys until sunset then cleaned up and headed for home. This is the life Buck had dreamed of, the worries of murders could fade for just one day. Tomorrow would be soon enough for him to get back to it.

15 BUCK AWOKE TO the sound of the telephone at 2 a.m. The night dispatcher said he thought Buck should come right away. There'd been a break in at the library and the back of it had caught fire. The fire department had it pretty well out. Buck dressed quickly.

"What is it?" Ruth asked sleepily.

"Fire at the library. They have it out. I'm going to see what's going on. It must tie in with Miss Emily somehow. You go back to sleep, I'll be home for breakfast." He leaned over the bed and kissed her on the cheek.

Buck wasted no time in getting to the library. The fire had been contained to the old storeroom at the back. Fire chief Ron Waters had the fire out and his crew was trying to figure out what had started it.

Ron had been two years younger than Buck in high school, but his excessive weight gain made him look ten years older. His once thick hair was balding and what remained was completely white. He'd been the fire chief for about fifteen years. It was Ron who called Buck when the Chief's job came open.

"Got the fire out, Buck. Looks like there was a break in and somebody was trying to cover it up."

"Thanks, Chief. Do you know what was used to start the fire?"

"Plain old lighter fluid. Found the can in the rubble. Don't think there was much damage in the library other than smoke. We caught it before the sprinkler system went off."

Buck shook his head, "Be a real shame to lose both the librarian and the library within a week of each other. There has to be something here I'm missing."

"There's not much you can do here. Might as well grab yourself a cup of coffee or just go back home to bed."

"Think I'll stop in at the office, grab coffee, and go over what I know."

"Okay, I'll get any information to you there."

The dispatcher looked up as Buck walked in. "Josh Decker was here just a few minutes ago."

"What did he want?" Buck asked disgustedly.

56

"Seems he wanted to know if you were at the scene. He was looking for a comment. Told him he'd have to ask you."

"Good, if he comes back, I'm not in."

Buck went to his office and pulled out his notes. This case had more twists and turns than a mountain road. He wondered how the break in and fire connected to Miss Emily. Or was it just some petty vandalism? Somehow, he didn't think so. As he looked at his list, he wondered just what it was he was missing. There had to be something.

Buck quickly walked out to the dispatcher. "Have we got someone who can cruise by the Meeks' house?'

"Should have. No one is needed for crowd control at the library."

"Send two cars. Be sure they get out a do a walk around. If the library fire had anything to do with Miss Emily's death, they may go back to her house and try to break in. I don't want to see it go up in flames."

"Sure thing, Buck." He picked up the radio and immediately sent two cars to check out the Meeks' house. He also suggested they might want to cruise by it regularly tonight.

"Good thinking," Buck acknowledged. He poured himself a cup of stale coffee and went back to his notes. Yep, this was a puzzling case. Again, Josh Decker was on top of things. *What was his connection? Did it have to do with his past?* Buck just couldn't figure it. He had never liked Decker, but he didn't see him as a killer. Maybe he'd been away from violent crime too long, maybe he'd lost his edge. He didn't think so, but it was possible. The more he learned the more questions he came up with. *What was he missing? What was the link?* He really needed to talk to Rick Brinks at the bank. The key might be where the money came from.

Miss Emily Meeks

Closed library 4:30 p.m. Saturday.

Where did she go from there? To see Mrs. Wilkes. Left around 6 o'clock. Arrived Grady's Market 6:15 p.m.

Did she attend church on Sunday? No

Who saw her last? Taxi driver??

Did she make any phone calls? NO

Who is the next of kin? DAUGHTER, Ella Mitchell, River City, seems broken up

Where is Dewey the cat?

What did she have? Could it have been $

Who ransacked the house?

What did they want?

Who ransacked the library?

Did they find what they were looking for? *Possibly not*

How did Miss Emily die? **MURDER**

What made her last moments so horrible? **POISON** — conscious, knew she was dying

What kind of poison was it? *Gelsemium-paralytic, leading to painful death*

When did she die? Sunday morning between 4 and 4:30 a.m.

Who killed her and *why*? Was it for the money?

Where did the money come from?

What's in the safe deposit box?

Secrets? Miss Emily had daughter, Miss Emily had millions. Josh Decker has criminal record.

Why does Josh Decker keep turning up? Has a criminal background, was seen talking to Miss Emily in grocery store.

Who is in the will?

Why was Josh Decker taking pictures at the funeral?

Why was there a second attempt to break in at the library?

Who started the fire?

What did it have to do with Miss Emily?

Buck put the file away and did some paperwork he'd been neglecting. Finally, at 5:30 a.m. he closed his office and headed for home. He stopped at the bakery to see if Mrs. Maxwell had anything ready yet. He knew she'd been in for almost an hour getting things ready for the new day. She officially opened to the public at 6 a.m., but Buck knew he could go in the back door and she'd fix him up. She'd been fixing him up since he was a kid.

Martha Maxwell looked up from the sink as she heard the back-door open. She was not surprised to see Buck Wise coming through the door. He'd been coming in the back door for as long as she could remember. She was somewhere in her late sixties with white hair and a good nature. Buck had always been one of her favorites. He kept her lawn mowed in the summer, while she worked long hours. Even now he took care of the heavy yard work for her.

"This fire at the library is not so good, Buck. I should maybe start locking my back door," she said as he approached.

"It might not be a bad idea, Mrs. Maxwell. We seem to have a rash of crime right now."

"Somehow, I think when you learn who killed Miss Emily, we will not have crime," she said thoughtfully.

Buck nodded, "I think you are right."

"So, what can I do for you this morning? Are you taking donuts to the office?" she asked cheerfully.

"Nope, I'm heading home from the office, thought I'd surprise Ruth and the boys with a treat."

"I got just the thing. These cinnamon pull-a-parts just came out of the oven. I can pack them in a thermal box for you, keep them warm."

"Sounds great!" said Buck enthusiastically. "How much do I owe you?"

"For you $3.00 special," she said with a wink.

He gave her a five and said, "Keep the change."

She smiled and laughed. Buck left by the backdoor whistling.

At home, he put the coffee on and started making breakfast. Ruth came in all showered and ready for her first cup of coffee.

"How bad was it?" she asked.

"Not bad," he answered, "almost seemed like it was set as a diversion. Everything else in town is quiet though. I did send a couple of guys out to walk the grounds at the Meeks place. I didn't want to risk a break in there when I'm getting ready to turn it over to the daughter."

"A wise thing to do. Do you think the fire had to do with Miss Emily's death?"

"Can't say."

"Can't say or won't?"

Buck paused to look at his wife, "I truly can't say. I don't know."

"Well, I sure hope not. We left the city to get away from this kind of thing."

"Let me do the worrying."

Just then, the boys came rushing in, "How come Dad is cooking breakfast?" Joey demanded.

"I was up early this morning and wanted to give your Mom a break," he replied. "Might want to look in the box on the table."

Both boys headed for the table, each wanting to be the first to get to the box. Ruth beat them both. She gently opened the box.

"Cinnamon pull-a-parts!" Jake shouted. "Dad, this is great!"

The table was quickly set. Buck put eggs and toast on everyone's plate. Each helped themselves to a pull-a-part. Ruth got the juice and they set down to enjoy breakfast together.

16 AFTER BREAKFAST, BUCK took a shower, dressed, and then drove to the bank. He wanted to know where the money came from. He wanted to know if it was still coming in. Buck wasn't going to leave with out answers.

Rick Brinks saw Buck enter and hurried from his office to greet him. He didn't want people to think there was something wrong at the bank. Image was everything.

"Good Morning, Chief. Can I assist you this morning?"

Buck smiled broadly, "Yes, we need to discuss those deposits you were checking for me."

"Come right this way. I have those records in my office." Brinks led the way to his office. Stopped to tell his secretary he was not to be disturbed and closed the door behind them. Once the door was closed, he hissed, "Was it necessary to come in here? I would have had them delivered to you today."

"Rick, after the fire last night, I needed them sooner than later. I decided to come get them myself. I knew you wouldn't want me to send the storm troopers in to disrupt business today." Buck put his hand to his face to cover a grin.

The banker looking chagrinned said, "No, you're probably right."

"Well, then, let's get to it. What can you tell me about the deposits?"

He thumbed through some papers and then said, "It seems they came from a company called Eco-World. It's based in New York City."

"Is this a company concerned with our eco-system?" Buck asked. "Do we have a name of a person signing the checks?"

"Chief," Brinks said bristling, "it's what this town pays you to do. I found out what I could."

"Just a couple more things," said Buck. "How much were the checks and how often did they come?"

"They came twice a month in the amount of $5,000 each."

"Are they still coming?"

"No, they stopped coming about six years ago."

"Thanks, for your time," Buck said as the banker handed him the folder. "I'll let you know if I have any more questions."

"You do *that*," said Brinks sarcastically.

The two men shook hands and Brinks put on his smiling banker face and walked Buck to the door.

Buck was very thoughtful when he got back to the office. Millie handed him a copy of the fire chief's report and he headed for his office to determine today's work.

First, Buck looked at the bank records. Miss Emily was getting $10,000 dollars a month. She'd been getting it for twenty-six years. Alone it amounted to $3,120,000 dollars. How did she end up with over five million? It was a question for an accountant.

Buck picked up the phone and buzzed Millie, "Millie, can you get Stan Smyth on the line?"

"Sure thing, Buck."

It took less than three minutes for Millie to let Buck know she had Stan on line one.

"Buck, what did I do now to the chief is calling me first thing in the morning?" he said jovially.

"I need your help. I have some bank records I don't understand. Do you think you could drop by today?"

"Sure, how about right after lunch? I could be there say 1:15."

"Great. See you then."

"Looking forward to it."

Buck buzzed Millie again. "Millie, I need you to call Tom, Sr. and ask him to get us a subpoena for Miss Emily's safe deposit box. And I need it sooner than later."

"Ok, I'll get right on it."

Buck picked up the file from last night's fire. It was pretty much just what he suspected. Someone tried to break into the back of the library and when they couldn't get past the new locks, they started a diversionary fire. He still wondered what they thought they would find in the library.

The morning passed in a flurry of paperwork then Buck made his way to the Oak Grove Cafe for lunch. He chatted with the staff, enjoyed his meal, and walked back in time to meet Stan Smyth coming up the sidewalk to the police station.

"Afternoon, Buck," said Stan with a smile.

"Afternoon, glad you could come by."

The two men entered the police station and headed toward Buck's office. "Go on in and have a seat," said Buck. He stopped at the desk to see if Millie had any messages for him.

"No messages but, Tom, Sr. has a subpoena being delivered here in about an hour."

"Good, I want to know when it gets here and I'll take Tom, Jr. with me to serve it." Tom Haliday, Sr. had been the prosecutor for two and a half decades, his son, Tom, Jr., was a part-time deputy and a part-time coroner assistant. Both men were honest and fair and could be counted on to get the job done.

Buck stepped into his office. "Well, Stan, this could take a while. I need you to help me understand how Miss Emily ended up with five million in the bank and no one in town being any wiser."

"Let's have a look at the statements the bank gave you." Buck handed Stan the file. He studied it for a minute. "Well, I see you figured out where three million came from. Now you need to look at Miss Emily's personal deposits. Looks like she deposited most of her paycheck every two weeks. Hold on while I get my calculator."

He did some quick figuring and looked up. "Well, her income deposits equaled another half million. Which brings us to three point six million. Add the interest over the years, which would come to quite a bundle. I see she made a deposit of one hundred thousand about the time her father passed away, which would most likely have been inheritance. Give me a minute here and I'll see what else I can find."

Buck was content to watch Stan work. He knew what to look for and was efficient at it.

"Ah, ha!"

"What did you find?" Buck asked eagerly.

"It seems when her mother died everything was left to Miss Meeks."

"And?" Buck asked anxiously.

"And not counting the house, the tidy little sum looks to have been in the range of seven hundred fifty thousand; however, I can see where she used some of it over the years. Which accounts for where the money came from."

"Ok, now what do you know about a company called Eco-World?" Buck asked.

"Not a thing, why do you ask?"

"Seems the checks Miss Emily received were from them."

"I can make a few calls and get back to you later today or early tomorrow."

"Great, Stan. Thanks again for coming in."

The two men shook hands and Buck walked out with Stan. His timing was perfect, as Tom, Jr. had just come in with the subpoena for Miss Emily's safe deposit box.

"Stan, can you spare a few more minutes?" Buck asked.

"Sure, what do you need?"

"Tom and I are going to check the contents of Miss Emily's safe deposit box. There will be a bank official there along with Tom and me. I wouldn't mind an extra set of eyes, one with some financial background."

"I'd be happy to," Stan replied.

The three men walked the distance to the bank. Rick Brinks almost went into apoplexy when he saw the men enter. He quickly came toward them.

"What can I do for you three gentlemen this afternoon?" he asked nervously.

Buck quietly handed the subpoena allowing access to Miss Meeks' safe deposit box to the banker.

Brinks looked at the subpoena and said, "Right this way, Gentlemen."

The men all walked toward the back of the bank. Brinks motioned to his secretary to join them. She got up from her desk and trailed the men to the vault area. Brinks took a ring of keys off from his pocket. The secretary also had a ring of keys. They led the men to a private room, and then went to open the safe deposit box. Buck went with them.

Once the box was removed from its vault, Brinks carried it to the room. "Nothing else now, Margaret," he said dismissing his secretary. Margaret turned and left closing the door behind her. Plainly she was not pleased to be left out of whatever discovery the men made. With the door firmly closed the banker slowly opened the box.

17

LYING ON THE top was a long manila envelope addressed to Ben Wallace. Buck swore and turned to Tom, Jr. and said, "Get the car and go pick up Ben Wallace. Get him here pronto. We aren't touching a thing until he gets here."

Tom left and Rick Brinks spoke up, "I don't have all day for this Chief. We need to get on with it. I have a bank to run."

"Feel free to go and run your bank, Stan and I will be right here," Buck replied.

I can't leave the two of you here alone!" screeched the banker. "How do I know you won't touch anything?"

"You're accusing us of being thieves?" Stan asked incredulously.

"Well, I… uh, er… no," blustered Brinks.

"What exactly are you saying, Brinks?" demanded Buck.

"I…just I really do need to make sure things are running smoothly in the rest of the bank," he stammered.

"You knew when we came this was going to take a while. Everything in this box has to be logged. You must verify the log. Stan, here and Tom, Jr. will act as witnesses. This is standard police procedure," explained Buck. "How did you think the bank was going to survive while we did this?"

"Well, this is just so unexpected," he replied.

"Actually, the mistake was mine. I should have thought to bring Ben Wallace along in the first place. I knew he was Miss Emily's lawyer," Buck said apologetically.

The men stood awkwardly for a couple of minutes. Finally, Stan broke the silence saying, "I don't know about you two, but I'm going to make myself comfortable." So, saying he pulled out a chair and sat down.

Both Rick and Buck pulled out chairs and sat. Buck began filling out the top of the form, name of victim, date, people present, and reason for opening the box.

It was less than ten minutes and Tom appeared with Ben Wallace. The men shook hands and the process of going through the safe deposit box began. Buck handed the envelope to Ben. Ben opened it and began reading. He scanned it quickly and looked at the men gathered there.

"I suppose you will all hear this sooner or later, you might as well hear it now. Then we need to decide just how much of this leaves this room."

The men nodded, and Buck said, "We will not let one word leave this room until we have all the facts and have put the murderer of Miss Emily behind bars."

"I can agree," said Stan.

"Me, too," agreed Tom.

All eyes turned to Rick Brinks who said, "Well, of course I can be counted on. I'm a banker after all. Confidentiality is my motto."

Since it was agreed, Ben looked at the paper in his hand and began to read, his voice breaking only once during the narration. All the men were silent, each deep in his own thoughts.

My dearest Ben,

If you are reading this, I have died. Please do not be offended at the secrets I have kept. We have been friends too long for me to want to hurt you at this late date.

You have known for three years, I have a daughter; however, you do not know the whole story. I want you to know it now. It will be up to you to decide if Ella should know the story.

It was my senior year of college. I was already making plans to stay the following year and complete my Master's Degree. I was taking an economics class from this dynamic young professor. All the girls were starry-eyed over him. I was just interested in getting through the class. Economics was not a subject I found interesting, but it was required. The professor's name was Samuel Masterson. Yes, Senator Sam Masterson of New York. He is the CEO of Eco-World, a company he founded after leaving the teaching profession. He was very good looking and suave if you liked his type. I didn't particularly.

We were about half way through the course when I was summoned to his office. He talked to me about the class and my work in the class. He was disappointed I was not more enthusiastic about economics as I had the highest grade in his class. He suggested maybe we should have dinner one night and discuss it more. He was not pleased when I told him I didn't date professors. I believed it was not in either of our best interests. I think it led to what happened next.

It was a couple weeks later and I was finishing up a paper at the library. Professor Masterson passed by the table I was working at and stopped for what seemed to be friendly chat, just a professor saying hello to a student. I didn't think much of it and went back to my studies. It was late when I left the library. I had worked late at the library many nights and didn't feel threatened walking back to my dormitory. I knew I had to be in before curfew and had never missed.

This night was to be different. Professor Masterson stepped out of the shadows and blocked my path. When I attempted to go around him, explaining I could not miss curfew, he laughed and pulled me into the shadows. He started kissing me and pawing at me. When I tried to push him away and told him to stop he became more aggressive. I have no idea how we ended up on the ground. I just remember he was on top of me. The rest of the ordeal you can guess. When he finished, he told me, he expected me to be in his office the next evening so we could straighten out our differences and he wouldn't have to go to the Dean about my conduct, I was terrified. He was an important professor and I was just a student. He walked away and left me there. I was devastated. I slipped into the back door of the library and into the nearest restroom. I tried to clean myself up. When the library closed, I slipped into one of the listening rooms and hid in a corner. It's where I was when Mrs. Murray found me the next morning. I had gone into shock and could not speak. She called my housemother, Mrs. Jacobs, who came to get me. They took me out a back door and took me home.

Once home, instead of scolding me for missing curfew, she ran a hot bath and got me into it. She mixed me something soothing and tucked me into bed. She never asked any questions and I didn't speak. I awoke in the afternoon and got dressed. I went to find Mrs. Jacobs. I had to let her know I had a meeting with Professor Masterson.

Ben paused. The room remained silent. He took a deep breath and continued.

Yes, Ben, I kept the appointment with him. I think I knew what would happen, but I didn't know what else to do. From then on for the rest of the semester he and I had an appointment each week. I think he thought I would come around to his point of view. At the last appointment, he had the nerve to tell me, he never expected I would be such a cold fish. He was sure his charms would have awakened the woman in me.

I was disgusted, both with myself for having submitted to his humiliation of me and to him for having put me in the situation. I was relieved to be coming home for the holidays. I was looking forward to seeing you again, dear Ben.

Imagine my disappointment to learn that you had stayed on to work over the holidays. Then I learned I was pregnant. I was mortified. I could not tell my parents. They would have been so ashamed. I went back to college and spoke with Mrs. Jacobs. She was not the warmest of women, but she had been so kind to me the night after what I call the "attack." She was sure it happened the night I didn't show up. She helped me to secure a place at a home for unwed mothers. She also helped me arrange to finish my last year and my Master's Degree as an independent study program. I did not have to be on campus often and people would not gossip. I worked hard and took as many classes as I could during the summer.

It was during the summer I learned Professor Masterson was leaving for New York in August. I had not seen him since my return. Mrs. Jacobs had been kind enough to get me his class schedule and office hours, as he had been such a help to me the previous semester (If only she knew). So, I had been successful in not being on campus when he was. I called his office and made an evening appointment to see him. He actually sounded pleased I had called. He told me how he missed our sessions. I wondered how much he would miss them once he saw me.

I arrived on time and had the thrill of watching all the color drain from his face. How could I let this happen he wanted to know? As if being pregnant was entirely MY fault.I patiently explained to him since he was 50% of the problem, he was going to be 50% of the solution or I was going to the Dean. He was stunned to think I expected him to take some responsibility.

I had come with an outline of what was going to happen. He was going to pay for my medical costs and the costs I incurred while remaining at the home. He would pay for the birth of the child. He would sign off all legal rights to the child and I would give it up for adoption. He would pay me a stipend for as long as I never had any contact with the child or I deemed he was no longer financially responsible for ruining my life. He was stunned. I had drawn up papers in duplicate. I had made good use of my library time finding the correct legal wording and everything. I think he thought I had consulted a lawyer. He signed both copies. He also gave me the cash he had with *him. I told him I would forward the bills to him and he could just take care of them. He agreed and I left. My head was held high and I knew I had a secure future.*

"The nerve of that man!" Ben said angrily. "I wish I had known. I'd have done my best to see he never harmed an innocent young girl again."

"I think we all would have done something," Buck agreed.

"You don't think a man of his caliber still thought of Miss Meeks as a threat do, you?" Rick asked.

"A guy with as much power as he has all over the world," Stan stated. "Any hint of scandal has the potential to ruin him."

"Isn't there something we could do now?" Tom asked.

"Let's wait and hear the rest. Read on, Ben, Miss Emily had something she needed to get off her chest," Buck said.

I had my baby early in September, a beautiful little girl. I now know what a wonderful woman she has become. I named her Ella for my mother. I was pleased her adoptive parents kept the name. I am very proud of her; she has not had it easy. I want her to have luxury. As you will know from my bank statements and the contents of this box, I did not touch the money from Sam Masterson. I felt it was tainted. I found someone out of town to help me invest it. What Sam Masterson did not know until about six years ago is, I am the largest shareholder in his company after him. He holds 49% of the shares and I hold 40%. He was angered beyond belief when he learned this.

Enclosed in this envelope are the papers he signed all those years ago, Ella's original birth certificate with Sam's name as her father, and the stock certificates for Eco-World. This should all be given to Ella. She has every right to know who her father is. Whether you decide to tell her how she came to be will be up to you. I know you will do the right thing.

71

You will also find the deed to my house, and the jewelry belonging to my mother and grandmother. I am not sure if it has any real value; however, it should belong to my daughter.

The last letter from Sam Masterson is also here. It details how he intends to stop making bi-monthly payments to me. I smile when I think of how angry he must have been, I used everything I learned in his economics class to turn the tables on him.

The thing in life I truly regret, my dearest Ben, is not being honest with you. I have loved you since we were teens. I did not feel I could tell you because of what happened between Sam Masterson and me. I was no longer pure. I had been shamed and I felt I would have been a shame to you. Please forgive me. I hope you will come to know my Ella and her family. She is the daughter we should have had. Also, she will need a good lawyer to sort this all out.

As ever,

Emily

There was silence in the room when he finished. Finally, Rick Brinks said, "Let's get this inventoried. I have a bank to run."

"This isn't about you," Ben said angrily. "This is about a young woman who was ruined by a powerful man. What we do after we leave this room will affect many lives."

"Ben is right," Stan said. "Let's do the inventory and turn this stuff over."

"I'm in agreement," said Buck.

They quickly inventoried the box. They found the documents signed by Emily Meeks and Sam Masterson, Ella Mitchell's birth certificate, stock certificates amounting to 40% of the shares of Eco-World, and a box of jewelry. It was Rick Brinks who spoke next.

"The jewelry should probably be appraised to find out its value. Some of it does look as though it might be worth something."

"Rick is right," Stan chimed in. "Ella will want to know its value when she receives it."

"I'll take care of it," Ben said as he picked up a long slender box yet unopened.

"We haven't seen that box, yet," young Tom said.

"It's okay," Ben said, "I know what's in this one."

Buck looked at Ben and said, "We still need to log it in, Ben."

"It's a string of pearls with a diamond heart pendant," Ben said quietly. He opened the box. There lay the necklace, as it had been when he gave it to her all those years ago. He wondered what had happened to it. He'd only seen her wear it once after he gave it to her.

"Wow!" young Tom said.

"I guess we are finished here," Buck said quietly. "If each of you would sign your name on this inventory list, we can leave. Rick, do you have something Ben can carry all this in?"

"No need," Ben said. He leaned down and picked up his briefcase. "Once a lawyer, always a lawyer," he said smiling.

The others chuckled. They had agreed nothing seen or heard in the room would leave the room. Ella Mitchell would learn of this at the reading of her mother's will. Then each man left and Rick Brinks returned the box to its home in the vault.

As they were leaving, Ben said to Buck, "I'll call Ella today and set a time for the will reading and then I'll call and leave word with Millie."

Buck patted him on the shoulder and said, "Thanks."

Ben nodded sadly and the two men went their separate ways.

Tom, Jr. caught up with Buck, "What happened to Miss Emily was wrong, isn't there some way for her to get justice?"

"I think she found her own way to get justice," said Buck. "Uh, oh."

73

"What?"

"There's Josh Decker. How does he always know when there is something going on in this case?"

Tom said quickly, "I'm off. I've got my car just over there. Call me if you need me." He turned fleeing to his car.

"Chief, what was the meeting at the bank? Did you turn up something new on the Meeks case? Was the old lady hording contraband?" Josh Decker asked in rapid-fire order.

"I have no idea what you are babbling about, Decker," Buck replied as he continued on his way to the police station.

Decker fell into step beside him. "The meeting you and Tom, Jr. had at the bank with Mr. Wallace and Mr. Smyth. Did it have to do with the Meeks murder?"

"Mr. Smyth walked to the bank with me, but he did his business and I did mine. As to the others, I can only assume if you saw them in the bank, they were conducting their own business."

"Right. And you expect me to buy *that*," Decker said sarcastically.

They had arrived at the door of the station. "I'm not expecting you to buy anything. I don't know about any meeting. Now if you will excuse me, I have work to do." Turning Buck walked into the station and went directly to his office and closed the door.

Millie looked puzzled until she saw Josh Decker at the door. He hesitated, then turned and walked out.

18 MILLIE KNOCKED ON Buck's door.
"Come in."
"I see the press found you. What was he after this time?"

"Seems he thinks there was a meeting at the bank having something to do with Miss Emily's murder."

"Can't imagine how he knew you were going to be at the bank," Millie said.

"It sure didn't go out on the scanner," Buck replied. "I managed to brush him off, but I doubt he'll give up."

"Not if he's really a crook. I wonder what his stake is in all this mess?" mused Millie.

"I was wondering the same thing. Guess we'll just have to wait and see." Buck shook his head then added, "For someone so interested in the death of Miss Emily, he hasn't written one word about it in his paper. I find that strange."

"Yeah, come to think of it, I didn't see an obituary or anything," Millie said.

"Let's see she died over a week ago. The funeral was Saturday, and the whole town turned out and yet not a word in the paper. Nothing about the memorial on the steps or the attempted break in and the fire, makes me wonder," pondered Buck. "What is he up to? It's not just news reporting. I wonder who he's reporting to."

"Should I put a tail on him?" asked Millie.

"Not just yet," said Buck, "Can you get any more information on him? Where was he before he came to Oak Grove? I don't want criminal associations particularly. Maybe a call to his last parole officer to see if we can learn what kind of job he had."

"I'm on it." Millie headed for her desk to make some calls.

Buck pulled out his file and looked at his list. It was time he made some additions. He was learning a lot more. He might even be starting to put things together. Just as he started to write there was a hesitant knock at his door.

"Come in," he called.

The door opened slowly and in walked one of the Wilber kids. He carried a large box and his head was hanging.

Buck got up and walked toward him, "What can I do for you, young man?" he asked.

"Well, sir, I have come to turn myself in," the boy said dejectedly.

"And just what crime have you committed?" asked Buck amusedly.

The boy sat the box down and opened it. Inside curled up on an old ragged towel was Dewey. "I took him, sir, and he belongs to the library."

"Just when did you take him, son?" asked Buck.

"Two weeks ago, on Sunday. The library's back door was open and I snuck in. Dewey was hiding in a corner. Two men were knocking down books and makin' a mess."

"I'm glad you took Dewey. Do you know who the men were?"

The boy hung his head and shuffled his feet.

"It's okay, son, you could be a big help to me if you could tell me," Buck prompted.

The boy looked up then said, "I only knowed one of them."

"Tell me about the one you know."

"It was the newspaper fella. The one who's always askin' questions," the boy responded.

"Great! Can you describe the other man?"

"I think I could, but I ain't seen him around before," the boy said earnestly.

"I'll tell you what. I'm going to have Millie buy you a coke and then you can describe the other man to my computer man. He'll show you pictures on the computer and make the changes you tell him to make. When you are done, I'll get you a ride home in one of our cars."

"Ok," the boy said. "But what will happen to Dewey?"

"For now, I think it would be a good idea if you looked after him," Buck said. "Once we get a new librarian, we'll see if Dewey can go back to the library."

"You mean like I can keep him with me?"

"Yes," Buck said, "I'll make you one of my deputies and you can keep Dewey in your protective custody."

"Super!"

Buck walked to the door. "Millie, can you get young Mr. Wilbur a Coke and set him up with Andy, he's going to give him a sketch of one of our library bandits."

"Sure will, Buck. Come with me, Bobby, we'll get a Coke right now."

Bobby looked at Millie and down at the box with Dewey in it.

Buck sensing the boy was not sure what to do about the cat said, "It's okay, I'll keep him with me until you are done."

Bobby grinned and quickly followed Millie down the hall.

When Millie returned, Buck was standing in the door of his office, "Come here for a minute, Millie."

She walked to the office and Buck motioned her inside. He closed the door.

"What's going on, Buck?"

"Well, young Bobby came to turn himself in for catnapping Dewey. As it turns out he saw the two men who ransacked the library."

"He what!" Millie exclaimed.

"Yep, he saw them. He even knew one of them," Buck said with a sly smile on his face.

"Someone we know?" questioned Millie.

"None other than our faithful newspaper editor, Josh Decker," Buck replied. "So, I'd like it if you could get Tom, Sr. on the phone and get us a warrant for the arrest of Mr. Decker. At this point we just have breaking and entering, and vandalism. Tell him I'd like to reserve the murder charges just yet. Millie, we also need someone to keep a real close watch on the Wilbur place. I don't want anything to happen to young Bobby."

Millie stood and headed for the door. "And Millie, can you find me a badge?"

"A badge?"

"Yes, I told Bobby, I was going to make him a deputy and put him in charge of caring for Dewey."

Millie smiled, "I sure can."

Buck once again sat at his desk to make notes. Finally, some things were starting to fall into place. Buck felt that this murder would be solved sooner than he'd originally thought.

It gave him some measure of satisfaction things would get back to normal in Oak Grove. People would be able to feel safe again.

Miss Emily Meeks

Closed library 4:30 p.m. Saturday.

Where did she go from there? To see Mrs. Wilkes. Left around 6 o'clock. Arrived Grady's Market 6:15 p.m.

Did she attend church on Sunday? No

Who saw her last? Taxi driver??

Did she make any phone calls? NO

Who is the next of kin? DAUGHTER, Ella Mitchell, River City, seems broken up.

Where is Dewey the cat? Bobby Wilbur has him for safe keeping.

What did she have? Could it have been $

Who ransacked the house?

What did they want?

Who ransacked the library? Josh Decker and someone else

Did they find what they were looking for? Possibly not

How did Miss Emily die? **MURDER**

What made her last moments so horrible? **POISON**—conscious, knew she was dying

What kind of poison was it? Gelsemium

When did she die? Sunday morning between 4 and 4:30 a.m.

Who killed her and <u>why</u>? Was it for the money?

Where did the money come from? Sam Masterson

What's in the safe deposit box? Documents, birth certificate, stock certificates, jewelry, letter

Secrets? Miss Emily had daughter, Miss Emily had millions. Josh Decker has criminal record. Ella's father, Sam Masterson.

Why does Josh Decker keep turning up? Has a criminal background, Was seen talking to Miss Emily in grocery store.

Who is in the will?

Why was Josh Decker taking pictures at the funeral? Who is he reporting to? Where did the photos go?

Why was there a second attempt to break into the library?

Who started the fire?

What did it have to do with Miss Emily?

19 BUCK HAD ENOUGH for one day. He decided to head home to his family. Even though he never really talked about his cases, Ruth seemed to know how to help him unwind.

When he arrived home, he learned the boys had gone on an overnight campout with some friends. Although he would miss their banter and rough housing, he was almost relieved they were gone. He showered and changed and entered the kitchen.

He found the table with a linen tablecloth on it set for two. Candles were lit. It was something he and Ruth often enjoyed before the boys were born and did not get to do often. Ruth was fixing salad when he came in.

He walked up behind her and gave her a hug. "What did I do to deserve all this?"

She leaned into him and looked up from what she was doing, "I thought it would be a nice change since the boys were gone."

"Hmmm…it's a change. So, what are we having?"

"Aside from this salad, I have your favorite veggie lasagna in the oven with garlic bread. There is some wine chilling."

"Wonderful! How can I help?"

"Pour the wine and let me finish the salad."

Buck found two wine glasses and the corkscrew. He found a bottle of her favorite Running Red wine she found at a small winery on a trip they took to Tennessee a year ago. He opened the bottle, poured two glasses of wine, and carried them to the table. When he returned, she had the salad ready so he took it to the table. In moments, the lasagna and garlic bread were ready and they sat down to a quiet dinner.

Buck helped Ruth with the dishes and they took their coffee to the living room. He turned on the stereo and put in a CD by Yanni, one he often put in when he wanted to relax and get mellow.

He and Ruth curled up on the couch together and just listened to the music for a while. Ruth finally broke the silence to ask, "How was your day?"

"Well, I deputized young Bobby Wilbur. He is now officially in charge of Dewey, the library cat."

"Sounds like an important job."

"More than you know," Buck said seriously. "I have him reporting to Tom, Jr. every morning at 9 o'clock sharp and Tom is doing a drive by three times a day until further notice.'

"Buck, it sounds serious and a lot more like you are keeping tabs on Bobby than on the cat," Ruth said anxiously. She sat up for a better look at her husband. Then continued, "Bobby saw something having to do with Miss Emily didn't he?"

"Yes, and until I can arrest the people he saw, I want to know he is okay."

"Oh, my, does he know who was in her house?"

"No, I'm afraid he doesn't. But, what he does know is almost as dangerous."

"Oh," she said with a sigh. She leaned back against Buck's shoulder. She knew he'd told her all he could.

20 BUCK ARRIVED EARLY the next morning. He put in a call to Andy Hall. "Andy, did you get a usable face from young Bobby yesterday?"

"Yeah, Buck, he did a great job. I'm running it through an Image Ware program right now, as soon as I get a hit, I'll bring it to you."

"Thanks."

After he hung up the phone he put in a call to Tom, Jr. He wanted to have back up when he went to arrest Josh Decker. He wanted no trouble. Tom said he'd be in as soon as he swung by the Wilber place. He wanted to be sure Bobby was ok, since he'd be tied up when Bobby was to report in.

Buck made coffee and paced his office. When he couldn't stand it any longer he walked down to the bakery. Mrs. Maxwell came from the back; she was surprised to see Buck.

"Must be something wrong, you not coming in the back," she said jokingly.

"Just not myself this morning," said Buck noncommittally. "Why don't you put together a dozen of your delights and I'll treat my office."

Mrs. Maxwell quickly pulled together a dozen of her special donuts and creations. She also added one she knew was a favorite of Buck's. She put it on his department account and told him to have a good day.

He thanked her absently and walked out the door.

She watched him go and muttered to herself, "Something bad is going to happen."

Millie was at her desk when Buck got back to the office. She brightened when she saw the box from the bakery. Mrs. Maxwell made the best-baked goods.

Buck took the box to the coffee table and put it down, and then he headed for his office. Millie knew from experience Buck was worried about the arrest of Josh Decker. She also knew not to bother him unless it was urgent.

Buck jumped when his phone rang. It was on the second ring when he picked it up. "Buck here."

"Tom, Sr., Buck. I have the warrant you wanted."

"Thanks Tom, Junior and I will be there to get it shortly."

"Okay."

The phone disconnected in Buck's ear. Strange. He hit the phone's intercom button to call Millie and found it dead. Suddenly suspicious, Buck walked cautiously to his exit door. He did not want to open his office door and find himself under siege.

Once in the hallway he edged out the back to where he knew there would be a squad car. He quietly opened the door, picked up the radio and put out the following call: "This is

Chief Wise, need assistance at the courthouse. Prosecutor Haliday is being held hostage." Buck knew the person or persons in his office would hear the radio message. He quickly went to the front of the building to see who would be coming out the front door.

Tom, Jr. showed up outside the front door at the same time Buck did. "Is my dad okay?"

"He was a minute ago, I'm not sure about Millie though. Don't know who has the drop on her."

In the next moment, the door opened and Josh Decker shoved Millie out in front of him. Before he had a chance to look either way, Millie ducked and Tom, Jr. knocked the gun from his hand.

Buck took out handcuffs and said, "Josh Decker, you are under arrest. You have the right to remain silent. Anything you say can and will be used against you in a court of law. You have the right to an attorney. If you cannot afford one, the court will appoint one to represent you. Do you understand these rights as they have been read to you?"

Josh snickered. "Oh, I understand all right."

"Tom, take him in and lock him up. Have him sign the Miranda and get him a lawyer if he wants one."

"Sure thing, Buck."

"You ok, Millie," Buck asked as he reached out his hand.

She took his hand and he helped her up. "I'm fine. I sure am glad you put the radio call out. It really spooked him. He thought you were in your office and would just walk out."

"I knew something was up when the phone was disconnected."

"Well, now we have him, I'll rest a bit easier."

"I want to know who his partner is and what they were looking for." Buck said.

"Were they the ones who killed Miss Emily?"

"I don't know, but I doubt *'Mr. I'm Protected by the First Amendment'* will give us anything without a lawyer. Let's get back inside and get our phones back up."

Once the phones were up, Buck called Tom, Sr. back. "Tom, Buck here. Sorry we got disconnected earlier. We've got Josh Decker in custody."

"What do you mean you have him in custody? You haven't even picked up the warrant yet."

"The short story is he disconnected the phone while we were talking and took Millie hostage. Junior and I were able to apprehend him."

"Have you questioned him yet?" Tom asked.

"No. We read him his Miranda rights and tossed him in a cell. Thought I'd let him stew a bit."

"Good thinking. Let me know if I can be of any more help."

The two men hung up. Just then Andy Hall came charging into Buck's office.

"I've found him!" he shouted.

"Who?"

"The other man in the library. I also ran his rap sheet."

"Please tell me it's not someone we all know."

"Not unless you are keeping company with the New York crime families," Andy replied.

Buck sat up straighter, "New York crime families?"

"Yes, it seems our Mr. Decker's friend is from New York. He is connected to one of the crime families there. He has a reputation for being a leg breaker."

"Okay," Buck said reaching for the file in Andy's hand. "Let's get a good look at this guy and see what we're up against."

Andy handed him the file. He turned to go out the door, and then said, "It's a good thing Bobby was at the library on Sunday."

"Yes, it is."

Andy left and Buck opened the folder to read.

21

THE FACE INSIDE the folder was the face of Anthony Micelli a known strong arm in the Luigi family. He had several arrests for assault, a couple arrests for B and E, one conviction for assault; he served four years in up state New York before being paroled. He was a real piece of work. Buck did not remember seeing him around.

He picked up the phone and called the prison in New York. He asked to speak to the warden on a matter involving their former inmate, Anthony Micelli. He was connected right away.

"This is Warden Jones," said a voice on the other end.

"Buck Wise, here Chief in Oak Grove, Michigan. I've learned one of your former inmates might have been connected to a B and E we had here a couple of weeks ago."

"How can I help you?"

"I was wondering if you could tell me anything about his cell mates while he was in your custody."

"He had one cell mate for about a year, petty crook named Josh Decker. Decker had several aliases, do you need them?"

"No. I have them. I also have Decker in custody. Thanks for you time," Buck said.

"You're welcome, Chief, call me anytime." The warden disconnected.

This made sense to Buck. He called Tom, Sr. and had him draw up a warrant for Anthony Micelli. Then he had Millie wire the description and photo to neighboring police stations and put out an all-points bulletin adding he should be considered armed and dangerous.

When it was done, he asked to have Decker be brought into an interrogation room. He also suggested Ben Wallace might want to be present. Millie took care of everything and in fifteen minutes Buck found himself entering the interrogation room to begin questioning Josh Decker.

Decker looked up when Buck entered the room. He had loathing in his eyes as he watched the Chief.

Buck put a cup of coffee in front of Decker, then sat down across from him. Decker just eyed the coffee.

"I'd like to ask you some questions," Buck began.

"And I want a lawyer," Decker sneered.

"I have Ben Wallace just outside," Buck offered.

"I don't want that old coot," Decker said, "I want to make a phone call for my lawyer."

Buck got up and walked out. Decker picked up the coffee and took a sip. He leaned back and grinned. This was going to be easy.

Buck returned with a phone and plugged it in. He handed it to Decker and walked out again. Once outside, he hit a button on the wall which allowed him to listen to what was being said in the room.

Decker said into the phone, "I need to talk to the man. Tell him there has been a snag. Yeah, have him send me a lawyer." He then hung up the phone.

Buck walked into another room. "Was he on long enough to trace the call?"

"I only know he called a New York exchange. I couldn't get an exact number," Andy replied. "Sorry, Buck."

"No reason to be sorry. He's a slick one. He knew just how much time he had."

Buck returned to the interrogation room. Tom, Jr. was with him. "Take him back to his cell. I don't need him again until his lawyer shows up."

"C'mon, Decker," Junior said.

Decker rose slowly. He kept smiling as though he had a secret. "S'matter, Buck, you got no questions?"

"None until your lawyer arrives. Then we will go right to arraignment."

Buck walked from the room.

"Hands behind your back, Decker," ordered Junior. Decker complied and Tom put the cuffs on him. "Let's go." The two men left the room and headed toward the cells.

"What a waste of time," Ben said.

"Not at all," Buck replied. "We will have some way to connect him either to the Luigi crime family or Sam Masterson. We just have to wait and see who sends him a lawyer."

"Pretty slick," Ben admitted.

"Let's go get some coffee."

The two men got coffee and went to Buck's office. Buck took out the file he had on Anthony Micelli. He handed it to Ben who took the file and began reading.

Meantime, Buck called Tom, Sr. to bring him up to speed. Tom said he would prepare the proper papers for arraignment. He checked and Judge Alex Roy was sitting today.

Buck hung up the phone. He turned to Ben and said, "Tom says Judge Roy is sitting today."

"Good, Decker has no chance of bail," Ben said.

"What makes you think so?"

"Alex Roy is the only other man I know who proposed to Emily Meeks. He always had a soft spot for her. He will show no mercy to anyone who took a hand in harming her, and which includes making a mess of her library." Ben was smiling as he talked.

Buck nodded. He understood that kind of loyalty. For now, all they could do was wait.

2 2 IT WAS CLOSE to two o'clock when the call came in. Millie rushed into Buck's office.

"Buck, the sheriff's department just radioed in. They have our fugitive in custody. They'll be bringing him in shortly."

"Great! Get Ben Wallace over here. We may need him if the guy asks for a lawyer."

"Will do." Millie headed for her desk to make the call. While there she called Tom, Sr. to let him know what was happening.

It took less than ten minutes for Ben and Tom, Sr. to arrive. Both men wanted to be around for this interview. Millie took them to the conference room until Buck could take charge of the prisoner.

By the time, Millie returned to the front office, Buck had taken Anthony Micelli into custody and Junior was escorting him to an interrogation room.

"That was quick," she commented.

"The sheriff's deputies had all the paperwork ready, I just had to sign," Buck replied.

"So, what's next?"

"I'm going to talk with Ben and Tom, Sr. We may be able to arraign them both at the same time."

Buck walked down to the conference room and entered. Both Tom, Sr. and Ben began to rise. Buck motioned them to sit and pulled out a chair.

"Tom, do you think you can get charges ready for Anthony Micelli and get us before Judge Roy?"

"I've had papers tentatively ready since you first told me about him. I can have them done and waiting for me at the courthouse when I arrive."

"Good. Ben, I know this is asking a lot, but could you be in the court room in case Judge Roy has to appoint an attorney for Micelli?"

"Won't like it, but I'll be there."

"Okay, you two get things in motion. I'll be transporting these two in fifteen minutes."

"You decided not to wait on the New York lawyer, Buck?" Ben asked.

"Yep. I want to make sure these two don't slip away."

Tom nodded, "Good thinking."

The three men left. Tom and Ben headed for the courthouse. Tom pulled out his cell phone and made a call to his secretary.

Buck went to the front office. "Millie, get Tom, Jr. in here and Andy Hall." He continued to his office.

In his office, Buck checked his weapon. Tom and Andy arrived. Buck told them the two prisoners were going to be transported to the courthouse. Each man would have one in his car. The two men were not to talk to each other. Tom would leave first with Decker Buck would follow with Andy and Micelli.

"Treat them both as the most dangerous men you've ever encountered," Buck said seriously. "Tom, there will be a court officer with you and Decker from the moment you get out of the car. Andy, it will be you and I until I have to go into the courtroom. Are there any questions?"

As neither man had questions, Tom left to retrieve his prisoner and head for the courthouse. Five minutes later, Buck and Andy went to get Micelli and begin their short trip to the courthouse.

23 AT THE COURTHOUSE, Tom, Sr. and Ben were in the courtroom. Judge Roy was waiting to be announced. The Judge was a distinguished looking man, about six feet tall with silver hair and cold gray eyes. He was very imposing in his black robes.

Tom, Jr. and the court officer entered with Josh Decker in handcuffs.

The court clerk said, "All rise for the honorable Judge Alexander Roy."

Judge Roy entered and was seated He looked out into the courtroom and said, "You may be seated."

The clerk read the first case to be heard. "The City of Oak Grove vs. Joshua Decker of Oak Grove, the charges are breaking and entering, vandalism, and taking a hostage."

"Is their counsel for the defendant?" asked the Judge.

Before anyone could speak, the courtroom doors burst open and a squat man in a black suit came rushing in. "Excuse me, your Honor. I am Adam Saxon, Esquire, attorney for Mr. Decker."

"Approach," the Judge said.

Saxon approached the table where Josh Decker stood in handcuffs next to Tom, Jr. "Is this absolutely necessary?" he asked pointing to the handcuffs.

"It is," responded the judge.

"Might I have a few minutes with my client?"

"You may not. This is strictly an arraignment hearing. All I need from your client is a guilty or not guilty plea."

Josh Decker looked at the judge and in a clear voice said, "Not guilty, Sir."

"The people on bail, Mr. Haliday?" questioned the judge.

"Remand, you Honor. This man was seen breaking into the town library on the same morning the librarian was murdered."

"Mr. Saxon?"

"Remand is a bit high for breaking and entering," he said with conviction.

"Your Honor, the people would like to remind you, he took a hostage at the police station just this afternoon," Tom, Sr. put in.

"So, noted, bail is denied and the prisoner is remanded to the city jail until trial."

"We would ask for a speedy trial date, your, Honor," Saxon said.

"Mr. Haliday?"

"The people have no objection."

The judge looked down at his calendar. "One week from tomorrow at nine am sharp." He brought down his gavel and said, "Next case."

Decker was taken from the courtroom and Saxon hurried out the door behind him. At the same time, a second door was opened and Anthony Micelli was brought in between Buck Wise and Andy Hall.

Tom, Sr. nodded imperceptibly to Buck.

The clerk called the next case, "The City of Oak Grove vs. Anthony Micelli, residence unknown. The charges are breaking and entering a public building and vandalism."

"Is their representation for the defendant?" asked the Judge. Seeing no one move forward he continued, "As the bench sees Mr. Ben Wallace present it will impose on him to act as counsel for the defense until counsel can be provided."

Ben rose and approached the defense table.

91

Anthony Micelli blurted out, "I ain't bein' railroaded by some backwoods lawyer."

The gavel came down and Judge Roy spoke, "You will take this counsel until you can provide your own. Now how do you plead?"

"Not guilty."

"Mr. Haliday, the people on bail?"

"Remand your Honor, Mr. Micelli has no ties to the community and presents a flight risk. He was apprehended hitchhiking out of town by the sheriff's department."

"Mr. Wallace?"

"I concur, until I can speak with my client," was Ben's reply.

"It's a set up!" screamed Micelli.

The judge banged his gavel again. "Enough, Mr. Micelli, you are hereby remanded to the city jail. Should you wish other counsel, I will instruct Chief Wise to give you a phone to make a call."

Anthony Micelli was taken from the courtroom and returned to the city jail. He was given a cell in the south wing of the jail while his partner in crime was given a cell in the north wing.

24 BEN WALLACE ARRIVED at the police station with his briefcase. He asked to see the prisoner, Anthony Micelli. He filled out the appropriate forms and was taken to an interrogation room. He opened his case and took out a legal pad in preparation for consultation with his client.

Anthony Micelli was escorted in. His cuffs were removed. He sat down across from the lawyer. Micelli was a stocky man with a swarthy complexion. He had beady black eyes which quickly took in his surroundings.

"I told the judge I don't want no backwoods lawyer," he said insolently.

"Fine with me," Ben calmly replied, "I'll arrange for you to call someone."

He stepped to the door and tapped on it. An officer appeared. Ben explained what his client wanted. The door closed and Ben returned to his seat.

"Would you like me to do some preliminary stuff while we wait for the phone to come?"

"I ain't talkin' to you, old man."

"Suit yourself." Ben began to put his things in his briefcase.

The young officer returned with a phone and connected it. Ben arose and left with him. Micelli quickly dialed a number.

Outside the interrogation room, Buck and Ben listened to Micelli's side of the conversation.

"It's Tony. Put me through." There was a brief pause then he continued, "Send me an attorney. Yeah, I need to get sprung." He paused then added, "I need someone now before these rednecks railroad me." He hung up.

"Interesting," Ben said.

"Yeah," Buck agreed. He left and went to see if the trace on this call was picked up. He returned moments later smiling.

"We got this one?" Ben asked.

"Oh, yes," Buck said, "He called the offices of Eco-World."

"So, either he's for hire or Masterson is mob connected."

"What I'm thinking," Buck said. "I need to talk to Tom, Sr., but I think we're going to have to get the State's Attorney involved."

"Not only him," Ben replied. "You might have to look at involving the federal boys. This goes way beyond Emily's murder."

25

BUCK CLOSED THE office and went home. It had been a long day and he just wanted to be with his family. He puzzled over what had really happened to Emily Meeks. *Had a former lover killed her? Did she know something she hadn't divulged? How is Senator Masterson involved with organized crime?* It didn't make sense to Buck. The Senator was very vocal at wanting to put an end to organized crime in New York and the rest of the country. Now here it was right in Buck's backyard.

The boys were upstairs playing when Buck got home. Ruth had kept his dinner warm. Millie had called to let her know Buck was in court and would probably be late.

Buck ate at the kitchen counter. Between bites he said, "Don't look for the Gazette to come out any time soon."

"Why?"

"We arrested Josh Decker for taking Millie hostage."

"He what!" she exclaimed.

"Yeah, I think he was after me, but Tom, Jr. and I were able to apprehend him without anyone getting hurt."

"Well, it's a good thing."

"Yeah, now I just have to figure out his connection to Miss Emily."

As she cleaned up the dishes she looked at her husband and said confidently, "You will, Buck, you will."

He smiled and rose. "Think I'll check in on the boys, and then turn in." He turned and headed for the sound of laughter coming from his sons.

26

BUCK TOSSED AND turned all night. He awoke early and headed toward the office. Once there he put in a call to the Oak Grove Inn, the town's only hotel. He asked to be put through to Alex Saxon. The desk clerk said they didn't put through calls before nine o'clock. Buck who had not slept well and was looking for a fight informed the clerk an exception would be made this morning, to put the call through now.

Alex Saxon reached sleepily for his phone. "'lo," he muttered.

"Mr. Saxon, this is Chief Wise," Buck began, "We'll be bringing Josh Decker up for interrogation in thirty minutes. I thought you'd like to be here."

Saxon sat up in bed fully alert; "Thirty minutes!" he shouted, "That's unheard of, it's only," he looked at the clock, "6:00 a.m."

"I'm aware of the time, which is why I'm calling you," Buck stated.

"Well!" came the angry reply. "Don't you start until I get there." He hung slammed down the phone.

Buck chuckled as he hung up his end of the phone. He had one of his opponents up in arms, just what he was planning. He walked to the kitchen, picked out a cold cereal, some milk and a cup of coffee. On his way out, he grabbed a banana off the counter. This would be the morning fare for Josh Decker. He made his way into the north cellblock whistling.

Buck banged noisily on Decker's cell. "Wake up, sleepy-head, your breakfast is served," he said cheerily.

Decker rolled over and looked suspiciously at Buck. "Your lawyer will be here in thirty minutes. He's going to expect to see you fed and alert."

Decker groaned, stood and walked over to take the tray that Buck was holding.

"W's this? I'm supposed to get hot food," Decker whined.

"This," said Buck, "is what you get when I cook. The coffee is fresh." He turned to go.

"Hold up," Decker demanded, "I won't talk without my attorney. He isn't even coming here until nine."

Without turning Buck said, "He'll be here. I called him ten minutes ago."

"Argh," growled Decker.

Buck smiled and began whistling as he returned to his office. In the main office at her desk as usual was Millie.

"Thanks, Millie, for calling Ruth last night. I was so busy I didn't even think about it."

"No problem, Buck, just part of my job."

He stopped at his office door and looked at her, "No, Millie, it's not. Don't think I don't appreciate you looking after my family." He turned and went to his desk.

Millie just sat there for a moment. She remembered when Buck and his family came to town six years

ago. Ruth had taken and instant dislike to Millie on learning she dated Buck in high school. Millie, on the other hand, was jealous of the life Ruth had with Buck. It had taken close to two years to break down the barrier between the women. She now thought of Ruth as the sister she never had, funny how life changes things.

At 6:45 a.m., Alex Saxon entered the police station. He was huffing like he couldn't get his breath. Millie looked up and asked, "May I help you?"

"You most certainly can. Let me see Josh Decker immediately," he demanded.

"And you are?" she asked politely.

"I'm his attorney you, knit wit," Saxon said rudely.

Millie got up from her desk, her lithe five feet seven inches towering over Saxon. She walked to the desk and handed him some papers to sign. While he was signing, she said, "I need to see your identification for verification."

"Well," he sputtered looking up at her. He fumbled with his wallet to produce his driver's license and his card identifying him as an attorney.

Millie glanced at both and returned them. "Please take a seat and I'll have Josh Decker brought to a room where you can talk."

"Hmmph," Saxon muttered as he took a seat on one of the metal folding chairs gracing the office. He looked around, but found nothing of interest. He did note the woman took a great deal of time picking up the phone and requesting Decker be brought to a conference room. It seemed he waited forever before she spoke to him again.

"Mr. Saxon," she said quietly, "if you'll follow me, please."

Saxon almost jumped out of his chair. Making quite a bit of noise as he followed Millie to conference room three. She stood in the doorway. Saxon looked at her and said gruffly, "That'll be all." He attempted to close the door.

Millie stood her ground and said, "Chief Wise will see you both in ten minutes." Then she stepped back and allowed him to close the door.

27 "WHO DOES THIS small-town cop think he's dealing with?" Saxon complained.

Decker said nothing.

"Okay, Deck, what's going on? I got you took someone hostage, but what's the B and E stuff?" Saxon asked.

Decker said, "I got nuts yesterday. Was going to force the Chief to give me what he had on a local murder. He turned the tables on me and was arrested for taking a hostage. I have no clue about the B and E. Must be a trumped-up charge."

"Then, we should be able to get this cleared up in no time. Probably have to do some community service and pay a fine," Saxon said confidently.

Decker remained mute. He knew the locals better than Saxon did.

There was a quick rap on the door. One of the deputies opened it "Mr. Saxon, Chief Wise is waiting for you across the hall in the interrogation room."

Saxon rose, "Come along, Mr. Decker," he said.

"'Scuse me, Sir. I have to put the cuffs on the prisoner," the deputy said.

"We're just going across the hall," Saxon sputtered.

"Rules are rules, Sir," the deputy said as he moved to cuff Decker.

Saxon marched across the hall to the interrogation room. He opened the door to find Buck seated at a table. There was a small TV in the room and a tape recorder on the table. Millie was also seated at the table with a legal pad in front of her.

"What is the meaning of this?" Saxon demanded.

Buck rose to shake hands with the man, "I'm sorry, Mr. Saxon, just what is the problem?"

"Why, handcuffing Mr. Decker just to walk him across the hallway," the man sputtered.

"It's standard procedure for escorting a prisoner any place in my jail. Have I violated some right?" Buck asked innocently.

"Well, no," Saxon said, "it just seems a bit much."

The deputy entered with Decker and walked him to a seat and removed the cuffs.

"Is there anything else?" he asked Buck.

"Not right now, get some coffee and wait outside the door." The officer nodded and left. "Now," said Buck, "let's get to the business at hand. I would like permission to record this interrogation."

"Of course," replied Saxon, "as long as I get a copy."

Millie reached to the floor and produced a second tape recorder and set it on the table.

"What is that for?" Saxon asked.

"In the interest of saving time, we will use two recorders and you can take your copy with you when you leave. Also, there will be no question of tampering in the future," replied Buck.

"Get on with it," the lawyer demanded.

Millie turned on the two recorders and Buck spoke, "This is Buck Wise, Chief of the Oak Grove Police Department, Oak Grove, Michigan. Today is July 27th. In the room with me are Millie Wilson secretary, Attorney Alexander Saxon, and Joshua Decker. Mr. Decker is charged with breaking and entering and taking a hostage."

Then he began his questions. "Mr. Decker, can you tell me what you were looking for on the night of July 11th in the Oak Grove Library?"

"I wasn't there."

"Can you tell me what you and Miss Emily Meeks were talking about in the grocery store on July 9th?"

"Groceries, the weather. How should I know?" Decker answered.

"Allow me to show you a video," Buck said as he walked to the TV. He turned it on and pushed play.

Immediately on the screen was the scene of Josh Decker approaching Emily Meeks in the grocery store. Miss Meeks could be seen dropping a can. Decker spoke a few words, picked up the can, handed it to her, and walked away.

"Do you recall now what you were talking about?" Buck asked again.

"I have no idea," Decker said. "I probably just asked if she was okay."

"Why would she drop something at the sight of you?"

"How should I know? She was an old lady."

"Not so old," Buck replied, "just in her early fifties How well do you know Anthony Micelli?"

"I don't."

"You might want to rethink that answer," Buck said as he opened the file in front of him. "According to this, the two of you spent time together in prison in up state New York."

"Yeah, well, there were a hundred other guys in prison, too."

"A hundred other guys weren't your cell mate."

"Where are you going with this?" Saxon interjected.

"I have a witness who puts your client and Anthony Micelli inside the library on July 11th. I'd just like to know what they were looking for."

"Might I have a moment with my client?"

"Certainly." Millie turned off the tape recorders, then she and Buck left the room. They walked into an adjoining room so they could watch the two.

"He certainly seems sure of himself," Millie said.

"I don't think we're going to get much from him," Buck agreed. "I just need to see what they think they can offer."

"What about Micelli?"

"Decker thinks he's out of town. He has no clue we have him locked up."

"Do you think Micelli will talk?"

Buck pondered the idea then said, "Only to save his own skin. He'd willingly give up Decker in a heart beat."

The attorney knocked on the door. "There's our cue," said Buck. He and Millie rejoined Decker and Saxon in the interrogation room and Millie restarted the tape recorders.

"My client concedes he and this Micelli were cell mates in prison," Saxon began.

"Good," said Buck, "then he might be able to tell me what he and Mr. Micelli were looking for when they were tearing apart the library."

"I wasn't in your library," Decker said forcefully, "and I haven't seen Tony Micelli since I got out. I've got a new life now, a respectable life. I run a newspaper."

"It would seem it is what you have been doing for the past five years," Buck agreed. "However, I have learned you went to work on one of the papers owned by the Luigi crime family when you got out of prison. How did you earn enough money to buy the paper here?"

"I saved, just like everyone else," Decker smirked.

"Not exactly true," Buck began.

"Are you calling me a liar?"

"I'm saying you had some help with the financing of your newspaper."

"Just because I borrowed from Sal Luigi, doesn't mean anything. I've paid him back."

"And you have documentation that proves the loan is paid?" Buck asked.

"Of course, I do."

"You'll need to produce those papers."

At this point, Saxon spoke up, "Look, Chief, I'd like to see this matter cleared up and so would my client."

"Sounds good to me," Buck agreed, "How about getting him to honestly answer my questions?"

Saxon ignored Buck's question and continued, "Mr. Decker is willing to pay for the damage to the library. He will do community service to make up for his prank yesterday."

Millie gasped. Buck looked at the two men before him incredulously.

"I believe we are at an impasse," Buck said calmly. "Mr. Decker will be standing trial for the breaking and entering at the library, and for taking Ms. Wilson hostage yesterday. Neither of which are crimes which can be bought off and taken care of by community service," saying that Buck stood. Millie turned off the tape recorders. She handed one tape to Mr. Saxon and took the other. Both Millie and Buck left the room.

The two men in the room faced each other. Finally, Saxon said, "I'll make a call. We'll get some muscle in here and get this taken care of."

"You'd better," Decker said, "I don't like the accommodations here."

The young officer returned to handcuff Decker and take him back to his cell.

Saxon hustled himself out of the room and headed for the inn. He already had his cell phone at his ear.

28 MID-AFTERNOON HERALDED THE arrival of the New York attorney, Marcus S. Silverman. He was in his late forties, about five feet eleven inches and of slender build. He had the look of someone who spent much of his time indoors. His complexion was pale as were his blue eyes. His hair was more white than blond and lent to his ghost like appearance. He reported directly to the police station when he arrived in town.

Millie looked up when the door opened and the stranger approached. "How may I help you?" she asked.

"I'm Marcus Silverman," he said, "I've just arrived from New York. I understand you are holding Anthony Micelli, I'd like to speak with him."

"Of course, Mr. Silverman, if you would fill out these papers, I'll have Mr. Micelli brought to a conference room for you," she said politely.

Silverman began to fill out the papers and Millie called to have Micelli brought to conference room three. She walked back to the counter, saw the papers were in order and thanked Mr. Silverman for having his ID ready.

"Right this way," she said as she led the way to conference room three. "Mr. Micelli should be here in just a moment. Is there anything else you need?"

"Thank you, no," Silverman said dismissing her.

Millie closed the door and walked back to the front office. Buck was standing in the doorway.

"So, the mighty Silverman has arrived."

Millie nodded, "Much more polite than Saxon."

"Better breeding," Buck said with a chuckle.

In less than fifteen minutes, Silverman knocked on the door. He asked the young officer to find out if the Chief was available.

The young officer came to the front office. "Millie, the guy with Micelli wants to know if Buck is available."

"I'll check," Millie said as she picked up her phone and buzzed Buck.

"Buck here," he said when he answered.

"Mr. Silverman wants to know if you are available."

"Certainly," Buck responded, "set up the interrogation room again."

"Sure thing," she said as she hung up the phone. She turned to the young officer and said, "Buck will be right there."

"Thanks, Millie," he said and headed back to the conference room. At the door he rapped once.

Silverman opened the door.

"Chief Wise will be right with you."

"Thank you, young man," said Silverman. He closed the door and turned back to Micelli, "Don't say anything until I say so."

"Got it."

The two men waited. Buck arrived a few minutes later. He rapped on the door and opened it.

"You asked to see me?"

Silverman stood and extended his hand, "Yes, Marcus Silverman, attorney for Mr. Micelli."

"Pleased to meet you." Buck responded as he took the outstretched hand.

"I understand from my client you have not yet interrogated him."

"That is correct. He requested a lawyer, did not want the one appointed to him by the court. We have been awaiting your arrival."

"Very good of you. Can we proceed now?"

Buck nodded, "I have everything ready across the hall." He looked at Micelli, "Can you get across the hall without cuffs?"

Silverman answered, "I give you my word, Chief, there will be no problem." He nodded at Micelli, who rose and walked toward the door.

Buck opened the door and the young officer held open the door to the interrogation room across the hall. The three men entered and the door was closed behind them.

Millie sat where she had been during the interrogation of Josh Decker. The two tape recorders were already on the desk.

"If you don't mind, I'd like to record this interrogation," Buck said.

"Not a problem if I may get a copy."

Buck nodded, "We have two recorders, so you may take a copy with you."

"Well, planned," Silverman said with sincerity.

Millie turned on the recorders and Buck spoke, "It is July 27th we are in the interrogation room of the Oak Grove Police Department. I am Buck Wise, Chief of the Oak Grove Police Department."

Millie spoke next, "I am Millie Wilson, secretary of the Oak Grove Police Department."

"Marcus S. Silverman, attorney for the defense."

"Anthony Micelli."

Buck began his questions, "Mr. Micelli, what were you and Josh Decker looking for in the Oak Grove Library on July 11th?"

"Wasn't there."

"Mr. Micelli, I have an eye witness who can put both you and Decker in the library."

"Wasn't me. Ain't never been to Oak Grove until they brought me here yesterday."

"Mr. Decker says different."

"Don't know a Mr. Decker."

"Come, come," said Buck, "Surely you remember spending a year in a cell with Joshua Decker in up state New York."

"Deck, *that* little weasel? Haven't seen him in years."

"That little weasel as you so aptly put it says you've been staying with him for the past two weeks. In fact, hinted it might have been you who killed our local librarian."

"I didn't kill nobody!" Micelli yelled. "If that lyin' little varmint said I did, it was to save his own skin."

Silverman put a hand on Micelli's arm.

"What do you know about the death of Miss Meeks?"

"What's in it for me?"

"It would depend on what you know."

Micelli sat silently for a few minutes then said, "I need to talk to my attorney."

"Not a problem." Millie turned off the recorders then she and Buck left the room.

Not for the first time this day the two of them wondered what conversation was taking place in the next room.

"Do you think this one will ask for community service and a fine?" Millie asked.

"Nope," Buck replied, "this one has a much smarter lawyer. He wants to get this guy out of town."

"What do you think he's hiding?"

"Don't know, but I do know he wants to keep his association with Senator Masterson very quiet."

"You think Senator Masterson is mixed up in this?" Millie asked incredulously.

"More than you can imagine, Millie, more than you can imagine."

Before Millie could ask anything more, Silverman rapped on the two-way mirror.

Buck and Millie reentered the interrogation room. Millie sat and turned on the tape recorders.

Silverman began, "My client has some knowledge of what might have happened to your librarian. He can also tell you what Josh Decker was looking for, but he did not play any part in the woman's death. He only arrived at Decker's on Saturday before the library break in."

"I'm listening," Buck said.

Silverman nodded to Micelli. "I dropped in on Deck about 10 p.m. on Saturday. He said some old lady was hiding some important papers in the library. He asked if I'd help him find them, seemed pretty harmless, so I went along."

"Go on."

"We get to the library and go in through some back shed. Then the cat jumped at us, scared me half to death. Deck thought it was funny. We tousled a bit and knocked over a small book shelf. Deck said it was a good idea, I was to start tearing down books and he would go through the desk looking for the papers. Pretty much how it went."

"Did he find what he was looking for?"

"Don't think so. When he finished with the desk, he started throwing stuff all over the place."

"Did he suggest going to talk to the old lady?"

"Nope, I did, but he said it wouldn't do no good, cuz the lady was beyond talking."

"What did that mean to you?"

"It meant she was unconscious or dead. Either way she couldn't do no more talkin'."

"Thank you, Mr. Micelli," Buck said. "I'll take this tape to our prosecuting attorney and he'll contact Mr. Silverman to work out the details of your sentence."

Millie turned off the tape recorders and handed Mr. Silverman his copy. She took the other copy with her things and left the room.

Buck held out his hand to Silverman, "Thank you for your time."

Silverman took the outstretched hand. Buck left. Silverman hurried to catch up with Buck.

"Excuse me, Chief."

Buck turned, "Yes."

"Can you tell me where to find a room in this town?"

"Oak Grove Inn, just two blocks down and one block to the left."

Silverman nodded. "Thank you. Tell your prosecutor he can find me there."

Buck nodded and watched as the man left. Millie who'd been behind her desk said, "Buck, was way too easy, wasn't it?"

"Yep, sure was." Buck went to his office. He didn't know if he could make any sense of his notes, but he sure wanted to try. He knew more than he had earlier. He also had a hunch he wanted to follow up on. First, he would make his notes, and then he would go home, enjoy an evening with his family and get a good night sleep.

Buck pulled out the file marked Emily Meeks. He studied what was already written as he contemplated how to write in what he had learned. He also thought he'd be adding a few more questions. Before he started he reached for his phone.

"Tom, have you checked in on young Wilbur?"

"Yep, he and his charge are all safe and sound. Going to run by there once more before I go home."

"Thanks, Tom," Buck said then hung up the phone. The one secret he was keeping, he smiled at the thought.

Miss Emily Meeks

Closed library 4:30 p.m. Saturday.

Where did she go from there? To see Mrs. Wilkes. Left around 6 o'clock. Arrived Grady's Market 6:15 p.m.

Did she attend church on Sunday? No

Who saw her last? Taxi driver??

Did she make any phone calls? NO

Who is the next of kin? DAUGHTER, Ella Mitchell, River City, seems broken up

Where is Dewey the cat? Bobby Wilbur had him for safe keeping. I have Bobby safely kept.

What did she have? Could it have been $

Who ransacked the house?

What did they want?

Who ransacked the library? Josh Decker and Anthony Micelli

Did they find what they were looking for? Possibly not Decker wanted an important paper.

How did Miss Emily die? **MURDER**

What made her last moments so horrible? **POISON** — conscious, knew she was dying

What kind of poison was it? Gelsemium-paralytic, leading to painful death

When did she die? Sunday morning between 4 and 4:30 a.m. The poison had been given between 8:30 and 9:00 p.m. on Saturday.

Who killed her and *why*? Was it for the money? Decker????

Where did the money come from? Sam Masterson

What's in the safe deposit box? Documents, birth certificate, stock certificates, jewelry, letter

Secrets? Miss Emily has daughter, Miss Emily had millions. Josh Decker has criminal record. Ella's father, Sam Masterson.

Why does Josh Decker keep turning up? Has a criminal background, was seen talking to Miss Emily in grocery store.

Who is in the will?

Why was Josh Decker taking pictures at the funeral? Who is he reporting to? Where did the photos go? Why did the Luigi crime family send him a lawyer?

Why was there a second attempt to break into the library? There wasn't it only looked like one.

Who started the fire? It was all smoke. Something to get us looking elsewhere

What did it have to do with Miss Emily? Nothing other than to throw us off the trail.

Anthony Micelli??? Has an attorney from Eco-World and connections to the Luigi crime family. Says he only got to town about 10 p.m. Saturday?

Questions and more questions. Not many answers to go with the questions. Buck turned on his computer and went straight to Google. He needed to know where gelsemium came from. Once he had the information, he printed it, closed his file, locked up his office, and went to spend an evening with his family.

29 BUCK'S FIRST CALL in the morning was to Morning Side Nursery, they had supplied all of Miss Emily's flowers.

"Morning Side Nursery, this is Marge. How may I help you?"

"Marge, it's Chief Wise."

"Good morning, Chief, what can I do for you?"

"Do you remember when Miss Emily ordered her Carolina jasmine plant?"

"She never ordered one."

"You sure, Marge? She had one she kept in a small hot house."

"I'm sure. I've been selling Emily Meeks flowers since she was a kid and she never ordered a Carolina jasmine. In fact, the only person in town I know ever ordered any was the reporter fella, Decker and he ordered two."

"Thanks, Marge, you've been a great help." Buck hung up the phone having solved one mystery. The poison which killed Miss Emily came from Josh Decker.

Could Micelli have been telling the truth about when he arrived? Had Decker worked alone when Miss Emily was poisoned and her house ransacked? Things could be falling into place. Now might be a good time to talk to Decker and his lawyer again.

Buck picked up the phone and buzzed Millie, "Can you track down Decker's lawyer? I want to see if we can talk to him again. Get the last part of Micelli's tape ready to play, too." He waited for Millie's response then hung up the phone. Things were falling into place.

Buck needed Decker to tie in the Luigi family to Miss Emily's murder and Micelli to tie in the good Senator. He'd better call Tom, Sr. and bring him up to speed.

After talking to Tom, Sr., Buck knew in no time the State's Attorney General would be involved in this. He was also sure there would be some federal boys on his turf soon, too. This involved a US Senator and organized crime. There was no way Buck could keep it to himself and he was more than willing to take help.

Millie buzzed him when he hung up the phone, "Saxon says he can be here in an hour."

"Works for me, can you have the recording ready?"

"No problem."

"Good, let's go get some lunch."

Buck and Millie headed toward the Oak Grove Cafe. It was past the lunch rush so they knew they had time. They were greeted by waitresses and customers alike. Both ordered sandwiches and coffee, neither talked about business. Several friends joked they might have to tell Ruth Buck was

111

stepping out on her. Millie blushed, but knew it was far from the truth.

They found Saxon pacing the front office when they returned. "You're late," he bellowed.

"I'm sorry, Mr. Saxon, we do take lunches around here," Buck replied. "Millie, will you see to it Mr. Decker is brought to the interrogation room?"

"Certainly," she said as she reached for the phone.

Buck led the way to the interrogation room. They were all seated when Decker was ushered in.

"You called this meeting. Have you decided to agree to our terms?" Saxon demanded.

"I have something you should both hear," Buck replied calmly.

Millie turned on one of the tape recorders and the following was heard; "My client has some knowledge of what might have happened to your librarian. He can also tell you what Josh Decker was looking for, but he did not play any part in the woman's death. He only arrived at Decker's on Saturday before the library break in."

"I'm listening," Buck said.

"I dropped in on Deck about 10 p.m. on Saturday. He said some old lady was hiding some important papers in the library. He asked if I'd help him find them it seemed pretty harmless, so I went along."

"Go on."

"We get to the library and go in through some back shed. Then the cat jumped at us. Scared me half to death. Deck thought it was funny. We tousled a bit and knocked over a small book shelf. Deck said it was a good idea, I was to start tearing down books and he would go through the desk looking for the papers. That's pretty much it."

SECRETS

"Did he find what he was looking for?"

"Don't think so. When he finished with the desk, he started throwing stuff all over the place."

"Did he suggest going to talk to the old lady?"

"Nope, I did, but he said it wouldn't do no good, cuz the lady was beyond talking."

"What did that mean to you?"

"It meant she was unconscious or dead. Either way she couldn't do no more talkin'."

"Thank you, Mr. Micelli," Buck said. "I'll take this tape to our prosecuting attorney and he'll contact Mr. Silverman to work out the details of your sentence."

At the end of the recording, Millie turned off the player and turned on the second one.

Decker shouted, "That lying snake in the grass!"

Saxon interrupted before Decker could say anymore, "I think I need a word with my client."

Millie turned off the recorder then she and Buck left the room. From the other side of the two-way mirror, Buck and Millie got quite a show. Decker was raving like a madman and Saxon was trying to calm him to no avail.

"Looks like you got to him, Buck."

"That was the plan, Millie."

It took several minutes for Saxon to calm Decker. Once he did he started talking nonstop. Finally, the two men seemed to run out of steam. Saxon knocked on the door, and Buck and Millie took their cue to return.

Once everyone was seated, Millie turned on the tape recorders.

Saxon began at once, "Just what did you expect a criminal like Anthony Micelli to tell you? Did you think he would admit to breaking and entering as well as murder?"

"Not at all," Buck replied, "I do however have some other questions I'd like to ask your client."

"Go right ahead."

"Mr. Decker, how is it you happened to purchase two Carolina jasmine plants?"

"I have always enjoyed plants."

"Why is it you gave one to Miss Meeks?"

"She has beautiful flowers all around her home. I thought she might enjoy one." He smiled as if to charm them.

"Were you aware the plant was poisonous?"

"I heard that; however, Miss Meeks does not have small children so, I did not worry about it."

"Do you know what part of the plant is poisonous?"

"I don't recall or I never knew," he told them.

"What time did Anthony Micelli arrive at your home on the eleventh of July?"

"Early in the evening. I don't recall the time."

"Mr. Micelli believes he arrived around 10 p.m. Does that seem right to you?"

"It could be I wasn't looking at my clock." He was getting cocky now.

"At what time did you decide to break into the library?"

"I didn't break into the library. If Tony did, he did it on his own."

"I have an eye witness who places you at the library during the breaking and entering."

"Your witness is mistaken."

"At what time did you give Miss Meeks the poison?"

"I didn't give her any poison?" Decker insisted.

"What did you give her?"

"I gave her a cup of tea?"

"So, you were at her house the night she was killed?"

"I didn't say that!" shouted Decker

"You just said you gave her a cup of tea."

"Okay, so I was there." Decker shrugged.

"What time did you give her the cup of tea?"

"I don't know. Who was looking at the clock?"

"What were you looking for in her house?"

"I wasn't looking for anything?"

"Her house was ransacked and the next morning you were seen ransacking the library. What were you looking for?"

"I didn't ransack anything. I wasn't at the library," he insisted again.

Buck shrugged his shoulders. I believe those are all the questions I have for now. You talk with your lawyer and get back to me if you have anything else to add." Millie turned off the tape recorder and removed both tapes.

"I'd like a copy of both of those," Saxon said.

"They will be waiting for you when you are ready to leave," Buck replied. He and Millie left the two to talk.

Buck went to his office while Millie made copies of the tape and put them in an envelope for Saxon.

Saxon only remained a few minutes, before collecting the envelope from Millie and left.

30 BUCK HAD TO plan a strategy to get Decker and Micelli to give him Masterson and the Luigi family. He'd be happy if he could get Masterson, the Luigi's would just be icing on the cake. He pulled out his list to see what else he could add. He knew this last round with Decker had given him something. He just didn't know if it gave him enough. If only he could see what was missing. *The tea that was it! The poison was in the tea. Decker gave Miss Emily the tea…Decker was the killer.*

Now all Buck had to do was figure out why. What made Decker kill Miss Emily? How did it connect to Senator Masterson? How did it connect to the Luigi family? These were questions Buck still had to answer.

Miss Emily Meeks

Closed library 4:30 p.m. Saturday.

Where did she go from there? To see Mrs. Wilkes. Left around 6 o'clock. Arrived Grady's Market 6:15 p.m.

Did she attend church on Sunday? No

Who saw her last? Taxi driver??

Did she make any phone calls? NO

Who is the next of kin? DAUGHTER, Ella Mitchell, River City, seems broken up

Where is Dewey the cat? Bobby Wilbur had him for safe keeping. I have Bobby safely kept.

What did she have? Could it have been $

Who ransacked the house?

What did they want?

Who ransacked the library? Josh Decker and Anthony Micelli

Did they find what they were looking for? Possibly not Decker wanted an important paper.

How did Miss Emily die? **MURDER**

What made her last moments so horrible? **POISON**—conscious, knew she was dying

What kind of poison was it? Gelsemium-paralitc leading to painful death

Decker gave Miss Emily tea...poison was in the tea

When did she die? Sunday morning between 4 and 4:30 a.m. The poison had been given between 8:30 and 9:00 p.m. on Saturday

Who killed her and <u>why</u>? Was it for the money? Decker????

Where did the money come from? Sam Masterson

What's in the safe deposit box? Documents, birth certificate, stock certificates, jewelry, letter

Secrets? Miss Emily had daughter, Miss Emily had millions. Josh Decker has criminal record. Ella's father, Sam Masterson.

Why does Josh Decker keep turning up? Has a criminal background, was seen talking to Miss Emily in grocery store.

Who is in the will?

Why was Josh Decker taking pictures at the funeral? Who is he reporting to? Where did the photos go? Why did the Luigi crime family send him a lawyer?

Why was there a second attempt to break into the library? There wasn't it only looked like one.

Who started the fire? It was all smoke. Something to get us looking elsewhere.

What did it have to do with Miss Emily? Nothing other than to throw us off the trail.

Anthony Micelli??? Has an attorney from Eco-World and connections to the Luigi crime family. Says he only got to town about 10 p.m. Saturday?

It was then, Buck's phone rang. "Buck here."

"Ben Wallace, Buck. I have a time for the reading of the will."

"Great, Ben! When will it be?"

"Today at 6 p.m. Sorry for the late notice."

"No problem. Will it be ok for me to bring Millie?"

"It shouldn't be a problem. See you both then."

The two men hung up and Buck buzzed Millie, "We have a meeting in Ben Wallace's office at 6. I'll need you to take notes. He'll be reading Miss Emily's will."

"No problem. You want me to call Ruth?"

"No, I'll do it. You get ready and we'll grab some dinner."

"Oh, boy, lunch and dinner at the Oak Gove Café, everyone in town will be talking after this," Millie said with a chuckle.

"You let me worry about it."

Buck hung up from Millie and called his wife.

"Hello," came the sound of Ruth's cheery voice.

"Hello, yourself," said Buck.

"Uh, oh," she said, "you only call when something is up."

"Something is up, the reading of Miss Emily's will. Millie and I are going to grab some dinner and then head to Ben Wallace's office. I should be home by eight."

"Ok, the boys and I will make do without you," she said resignedly.

"Love you, hugs to the boys," Buck said.

"Love you, too," she said and hung up the phone.

Buck frowned as he hung up the phone. He wanted this case to be over. He wanted life to be normal again in Oak Grove.

31 BUCK AND MILLIE joined Ella and Matt Mitchell in Ben Wallace's office. Ben said it would be just a minute as he was waiting for one more person. After about five minutes, Henry Watson stumped into the room.

Ben introduced everyone and began the reading of the will:

I, Emily Sarah Meeks, being of sound mind and body do bequeath my estate to the following people. To Henry Watson, who has been a faithful friend, I leave $25,000. The rest of my estate will be left to my daughter, Ella Mitchell, with the provision $100,000 each be set aside in a trust for my grandchildren. The shares of stock go to Ella as the rightful heir to the Eco-World Company. It will be up to her whether or not she makes herself known to her father. I wish my estate to be managed by my appointed executor, Ben Wallace, who will treat it with as much care as he has given it in my life time.

Emily Sarah Meeks

Emily Sarah Meeks

Dated this 4th day of March, 2002

Witnessed by

Polly Watson *Polly Watson*

Benjamin Wallace *Benjamin Wallace*

Stella Osborne *Stella Osborne*

When Ben finished reading there was silence in the room. No one seemed to know what to say. Ben said he also had a letter for Mrs. Mitchell and handed her an envelope.

"I would understand if you want to take home to read it," he said kindly.

"Thank you," she said quietly as she took the envelope. "I hope you all won't mind if Matt and I go home now. The children are with Matt's parents and I'd like to be with them." They both stood.

Buck held out his hand to Matthew, "Take good care of her, son. We think of her as family." He then turned to Ella and gave her a quick hug. "You call me if you need anything."

Millie extended her hand to both Mitchells and then they left.

Henry Watson stood also. "I thank 'e, Ben. I'll see you in the morning about what to do with the money." Ben nodded.

Buck and Millie waited until everyone else had gone. When the door had closed, Buck said, "No real surprises there."

"No," Ben agreed. "I'm not sure how the will reading was any help to you."

"It helped just to know what Miss Emily had planned. None of them were suspects anyway. Thanks for letting us attend." Buck shook hands with Ben then he and Millie left.

"Do you need a lift home?" Buck asked.

"No, thanks, my car is behind the station," Millie said. "I'll see you in the morning."

"Thanks for coming along, Millie," Buck said.

He watched her walk to her car. When she was safely inside, Buck went into his office to close up for the day. Any more notes he was going to make could wait until tomorrow.

32 BUCK HEADED FOR the office still not sure how he could break Decker and or Micelli. There was something right there he couldn't see. He walked in, started the coffee, and then he headed to his office. This time he pulled out his list. He would find the missing link if it took him all day. All day was about all he was going to get. He had a message on his desk last night the federal boys would be in tomorrow.

Miss Emily Meeks

Closed library 4:30 p.m. Saturday.

Where did she go from there? To see Mrs. Wilkes. Left around 6 o'clock. Arrived Grady's Market 6:15 p.m.

Did she attend church on Sunday? No

Who saw her last? Taxi driver?? Who was taxi driver?

Did she make any phone calls? NO

Who is the next of kin? DAUGHTER, Ella Mitchell, River City, seems broken up

Where is Dewey the cat? Bobby Wilbur had him for safe keeping. I have Bobby safely kept.

What did she have? Could it have been $

Who ransacked the house?

What did they want?

Who ransacked the library? Josh Decker and Anthony Micelli

Did they find what they were looking for? Possibly not Decker wanted an important paper.

How did Miss Emily die? **MURDER**

What made her last moments so horrible? **POISON**—conscious, knew she was dying

What kind of poison was it? Gelsemium, a paralytic leading to painful death

Decker gave Miss Emily tea….poison was in the tea

When did she die? Sunday morning between 4 and 4:30 a.m. The poison had been given between 8:30 and 9:00 p.m. on Saturday

Who killed her and why? Was it for the money? Decker????

Where did the money come from? Sam MastersonWhat's in the safe deposit box? Documents, birth certificate, stock certificates, jewelry, letter

Secrets? Miss Emily has daughter, Miss Emily had millions. Josh Decker has criminal record. Ella's father, Sam Masterson. Decker got help buying newspaper from Luigi crime family.

Why does Josh Decker keep turning up? Has a criminal background, was seen talking to Miss Emily in grocery store.

Who is in the will? Henry Watson, Ella Mitchell and her children

Why was Josh Decker taking pictures at the funeral?

Who is he reporting to? Where did the photos go?

Why did the Luigi crime family send him a lawyer?

Why was there a second attempt to break into at the library? There wasn't it only looked like one.

Who started the fire? It was all smoke. Something to get us looking elsewhere

What did it have to do with Miss Emily? Nothing other than to throw us off the trail.

Anthony Micelli??? Has an attorney from Eco-World and connections to the Luigi crime family. Says he only got to town about 10 p.m. Saturday? Admits to helping Decker trash library

Buck knew he better find out who the taxi driver was. He didn't remember seeing anything in the file. When he went back, he saw he'd made a note to call Butch at the taxi stand, and hadn't yet done so. *No time like the present,* Buck thought. He reached for the phone and dialed the taxi stand.

"Taxi, how can I help you?" Butch's gravelly voice came on the line.

"Butch, this is Buck Wise. I need you to check your records for July 9th about 6:30 p.m."

"Buck, I don't have any records for July 9th after 5 o'clock."
"Why?"

"I closed up and went fishin'."

"Butch, could anyone else have used your cab?"

"Could be," Butch said, "it was parked out front on Saturday morning and I coulda sworn I left it in the back."

"Thanks, Butch, you've been a big help." Buck hung up the phone. He thought for a minute before reaching for the phone again. This time he buzzed Andy Hall.

"Hall, here."

"Andy, will you check with Bob Grady over at the market and see if he has any outside cameras? I want to know if he's got any video of the cab that picked up Miss Emily on July 9th."

"Sure thing, Buck. I'll get right on it."

Both men disconnected, Buck berating himself for not catching it earlier. *Was it possible Micelli was the taxi driver? Was it the link he was missing? How could he have been so stupid?*

Buck got up and went for coffee. He could do nothing now until he heard back from Andy. It was going to be a waiting game and time was running out.

Millie sensed Buck was worried about something. She'd seen him restless before. She only wished there was something she could do. Since she didn't know what it was, she kept her mouth closed and herself busy.

33 BUCK CONTINUED TO pace his office. He knew he made a serious mistake. If Andy couldn't get the video, or it didn't have what he wanted, he'd be sunk. It was such a stupid mistake. He would bust himself back to a beat if he could.

Buck was still pacing when his phone rang. He jumped then quickly answered it, "Buck here."

"I've got the video and I think I have what you want," Andy said eagerly. "I'm making a print and I'll be up to your office as soon as I have it."

"Thanks," Buck said, and then he hung up the phone. He could only hope Andy was right. Buck continued pacing.

Andy arrived fifteen minutes later. He knocked on Buck's office door.

"Come in."

Andy entered. "I think this is what you wanted," he said brandishing the tape. He put it into the VCR and turned on the TV. Buck came closer to see.

On the screen came the taxi pulling up in front of the market. Andy had been able to zoom in on the driver. There sat Anthony Micelli as big as life.

"Terrific!" Buck shouted. He slapped Andy on the back. This was the break he needed. "Andy, my boy, you may have just cracked the Emily Meeks murder."

"Thank, Buck," Andy stammered. He wasn't sure how to react. He'd never seen his boss like this before. He left the room before he embarrassed himself.

Millie heard Buck and rose to her feet as Andy made his exit. She knew Buck would be next.

Buck, as Millie had predicted, came to his office door, "Millie, find me those two out of town lawyers. I want to interrogate both of their worthless clients and I want to do it soon."

"Right on it, boss," Millie said as she picked up the phone. It was good to know things were going the right way for them.

Millie was able to reach both attorneys. Saxon tried to make an excuse to put off another interrogation. Silverman agreed to come right over. Millie had them bring Micelli to an interrogation room and readied the tape recorders and the TV. She knew this was going to be an interesting afternoon.

34

SILVERMAN ARRIVED AND was escorted to the interrogation room. There he found Micelli waiting. Buck and Millie came in as soon as Silverman was seated.

"This is a little short notice, Chief," Silverman began.

"Something just came to my attention and I wanted to share it with you and your client. If you don't mind, we will again record this interrogation."

"I have no problem with that."

Millie turned on the tape recorders and Buck began as before, "This is Buck Wise, Chief...."

Silverman interrupted, "We stipulate that those present at the first interrogation are all present for this one."

"Thank you."

"Mr. Micelli, can you tell me again, when it was you came to Oak Grove?"

"Saturday night."

"That would be Saturday, July 11th?"

"Yeah, I guess."

"I'd like to show you a video tape I have."

"Sure, go ahead, I like TV."

Millie started the tape. The date flashed July 9, 6:00 p.m. then the video of the taxi driving up to the front of the market. It was followed by a close up of the taxi driver. Millie stopped the tape.

"Now would you like to tell me when you arrived in town?"

"Your picture there says July 9th so I guess it was July 9th."

"You admit that you are the one driving the taxi?"

"Yes."

"Well, I can add grand theft auto to the charges."

"There wasn't no theft, I put the car back. No harm done. I even filled it with gas."

"Where did you take Miss Meeks when she came out of the store?"

"I took the old biddy home. She whimpered all the way."

"And once you got her home what did you do?"

"Nothin'. I took the car back and walked to Deck's place."

"Did you go with Mr. Decker to see Miss Meeks on Saturday night?"

"Nah, he said he could handle the old lady. I stayed at his place and drank some beer."

"Do you know what Mr. Decker wanted from Miss Meeks?"

"Just some paper 's all I know."

"What brought you to Oak Grove in the first place?"

"I believe those are all the questions my client is willing to answer at this time. He and I need to speak before there are any more questions."

"Certainly," said Buck.

Millie turned off both the tape recorders, she handed one tape to Silverman, and then she and Buck left the room.

"Are we really making headway, Buck," Millie

"Yes, we have him driving Miss Emily away. As far as we know, he is the last person to see her alive. We know he was here on a job for someone. If only I can get the 'someone' out of him."

"Do you think he'll talk anymore today?"

"I doubt it, but we can use the video and his answers with Decker. He might fold."

In the meantime, Saxon and Decker had been cooling their heels in another interrogation room. Buck and Millie joined them. This room had been set up with two recorders and a TV set also.

"It's about time," Saxon said angrily.

"I'm sorry, to keep you waiting, I was with another prisoner. I'd like to begin now to keep you from waiting any longer. Again, I'd like to tape record our meeting."

"Yes, yes, get on with it."

Millie turned on the recorders and Buck began as before, "This is Buck Wise, Chief of the Oak Grove…"

"Enough already," Saxon interrupted, "We all know who's here. Nothing has changed."

"Okay, let me begin by asking Mr. Decker if he can tell us when Mr. Micelli came to town."

"Sometime Saturday day night July 10th."

"And you're quite sure about it?"

"Yes."

"Millie, if you would please start the tape."

Millie rose, walked to the TV, turned it on, and started the tape. The date flashed July 9, 6:00 p.m. Then came the video of the taxi driving up to the front of the market. It was followed by a close up of the taxi driver. Millie stopped the tape.

"Now would you care to change your answer?"

"Seems ol' Tony made it to town a day before he said he did."

"And did Mr. Micelli stay with you the whole time he was here?"

"Yes."

"Did you know he was going to steal Butch's taxi?"

"I knew he was going to borrow it, yes."

"Making you an accessory to grand theft auto."

"There was no theft. We just borrowed the car and then put it back."

"Were you in the car when Miss Meeks got into it?"

"No."

"Did Mr. Micelli go with you to see Miss Meeks on Saturday?"

"No."

"What was it you wanted from Miss Meeks?"

"Just some old paper."

"Did she give it to you?"

"No, the old lady stopped moving and talking after she drank her tea."

"Did you know the tea was poisoned?"

"NO! I didn't kill her!"

"Where did you get the tea?"

"Micelli had it. Said it was some new kind."

"Where did Mr. Micelli get the tea?"

"I don't know."

"What was the paper you were looking for?"

"I don't know. I just know that I got a message from the family she had an old paper of Senator Masterson's they would like to have."

"Did you know what was in the paper?"

"No."

"Did you know Mr. Micelli was coming to town?"

"No."

"Did the family tell you how long you had to get the paper?"

"No. I didn't think there was a rush."

"Why did you decide to get it on July 10th?"

"Micelli was looking for it too."

"Did the family send Micelli?"

"No."

"Do you know who did send him?"

"No, but I know it's someone important."

"How do you know?"

"Tony's scared of him and no one scares Tony."

"Thank you, Mr. Decker, Mr. Saxon, I have no further questions at this time."

Millie turned off the tape recorders she gave one tape to Mr. Saxon and put the other in her file. Both she and Buck left the room.

Buck said, "I want to see if Silverman is still here with Micelli."

"Okay."

Buck walked to the other interrogation room. Seeing the guard was gone, he opened the door and found it empty, just as expected. He walked back to the front office.

"Well, Millie, time to close up shop and go home."

"See you in the morning, Buck."

35 BUCK FELT READY to face anything. He knew who killed Emily Meeks. He just wasn't sure who sent him. He had his crime family tie-in so he would turn that and Decker over to the federal agents. Decker was only the accessory to the murder. Someone else wanted Emily Meeks out of the way and Buck had a serious suspicion that he knew who. He just needed the proof.

First thing he did was send copies of the videos and recordings of the interrogations over to Tom Haliday, Sr. He wanted Tom to fill in the State's Attorney when he arrived. Buck planned to be too busy to be tied up to attend.

Then because he was feeling pretty proud of himself, he called Mrs. Maxwell and asked her to get a dozen of her baked delights ready for him to pick up. That done he took out his list and made some additions.

Miss Emily Meeks

Closed library 4:30 p.m. Saturday.

Where did she go from there? To see Mrs. Wilkes. Left around 6 o'clock. Arrived Grady's Market 6:15 p.m.

Did she attend church on Sunday? No

Who saw her last? Taxi driver?? Who was taxi driver? Anthony Micelli

Did she make any phone calls? NO

Who is the next of kin? DAUGHTER, Ella Mitchell, River City, seems broken up

Where is Dewey the cat? Bobby Wilbur had him for safe keeping. I have Bobby safely kept.

What did she have? Could it have been $ A paper of some kind

Who ransacked the house? Decker

What did they want? A paper about Senator Masterson

Who ransacked the library? Josh Decker and Anthony Micelli

What they were looking for? Possibly not Decker wanted an important paper.

How did Miss Emily die? **MURDER**

What made her last moments so horrible? **POISON** —conscious, knew she was dying

What kind of poison was it? Gelsemium- paralytic leading to painful death

Decker gave Miss Emily tea…poison was in the tea

When did she die? Sunday morning between 4 and 4:30 a.m. The poison had been given between 8:30 and 9:00 p.m. on Saturday

Who killed her and why? Was it for the money? Decker???? Micelli for a paper about Masterson??

Where did the money come from? Sam Masterson

What's in the safe deposit box? Documents, birth certificate, stock certificates, jewelry, letter

Secrets? Miss Emily has daughter, Miss Emily had millions. Josh Decker has criminal record. Ella's father, Sam Masterson. Decker got help buying newspaper from Luigi crime family.

Why does Josh Decker keep turning up? Has a criminal background, was seen talking to Miss Emily in grocery store.

Who is in the will? Henry Watson, Ella Mitchell and her children

Why was Josh Decker taking pictures at the funeral? Who is he reporting to? Where did the photos go? Why did the Luigi crime family send him a lawyer?

Why was there a second attempt to break into at the library? There wasn't it only looked like one.

Who started the fire? It was all smoke. Something to get us looking elsewhere

What did it have to do with Miss Emily? Nothing other than to throw us off the trail.

Anthony Micelli??? Has an attorney from Eco-World and connections to the Luigi crime family. Says he only got to town about 10 p.m. Saturday? Admits to helping Decker trash library

Yes, it was going to be a good day, Buck could feel it. When he was done, he walked to the bakery and entered through the back door.

Mrs. Maxwell looked up and smiled. She got the box she had ready for Buck and handed it to him. As he left through the back door she thought, *Things are going to be okay.*

Millie came in and found the coffee brewing and Mrs. Maxwell's box of goodies on the counter. This was either a good thing or a bad thing. Millie wasn't one to question it, she opened the box and retrieved her favorite pastry got a cup of coffee and headed for the front office.

She could see Buck working at his desk, his office door open. Always a good sign. He was not pacing or brooding. Things might be looking up. She got busy typing up a report of the two interviews last night.

The phone rang and Millie answered, "Police department, how may I help you?"

"Buck Wise, Tom, Jr. here."

"One moment, please." Millie put Tom on hold and buzzed Buck.

"Buck here."

"Tom, Jr. on line one."

"Thanks." Buck quickly picked up line one. "What's up, Tom?"

"Bobby Wilbur didn't report in this morning!"

"Have you been out to check on him?"

"On my way right now. I just wanted to give you a heads up."

"Thanks, Tom," Buck said, "keep me posted."

"Will do."

Buck slowly hung up the phone. He'd been careful not to mention young Wilbur. Neither attorney had asked for a line up, so Bobby hadn't had to come in. Maybe it was nothing. He'd wait to see what Tom found out before he pushed the panic button.

The phone rang again. Millie answered, "Police department, how may I help you?"

The panicked voice on the other end said, "I need help! I'm tryin' to save Dewey."

"You just hold the line, Bobby."

"Buck!" Millie yelled.

Buck rushed to the office door.

"Young Bobby on line one, he's requesting help."

"I'll get him, you stay on the line so you can send help."

Buck quickly picked up his phone, "What's the problem, Bobby?"

"They's two men at my house. I never seen 'em before."

"Where are you?"

"I'm at Wilson's gas station."

"You stay inside. I'm sending a patrol car to come get you."

"Ok."

"Millie, send that out officer needs assistance. I'm on my way. And send back up to Tom."

Buck raced out the back door to his cruiser. He started the car and turned on the siren. He shot out of the parking lot and headed the two blocks to Wilson's gas station. Bobby stayed inside until he saw Buck, then he picked up the box with Dewey in it and jumped inside the door Buck held open for him.

"I'm sure glad you could come, Chief."

"It's what we do when and officer is in trouble, Bobby."

Bobby grinned from ear to ear just to think he was an officer. Buck turned off the siren and made his way back to the station. He radioed Tom he had the package and to be on the look out for two suspicious men near the Wilbur place.

When they got to the station, Millie told them that Tom had radioed in about the two suspicious men. They were federal agents. They had gotten lost and were looking for directions to town. Everyone had a good laugh over it.

Millie saw to it that Bobby had a pastry and the office settled down.

36 THE TWO FEDERAL agents showed up about fifteen minutes later. Millie took them to Buck's office. She knocked on the door.
"Come in." Buck looked up as the door opened.

"Buck, these two gentlemen are from the federal government."

"Thanks, Millie. Come in gentlemen, have a seat."

The men took the seats offered by Buck. Both wore black suits, white shirts, and plain ties. They reminded Buck of a pair of paper dolls. Each one trim, one blond and one dark haired. Both had non-descript features and would blend in, except for the suits.

"How can I help you?"

The blond spoke, "I'm Robert Cotton and his is James Weston of the federal task force on organized crime. We understand you have something going on with the Luigi crime family."

"True. I'd be happy to fill you in on what's been going on and turn my prisoner over to you."

Buck spent the next hour filling in the two officers. He played the recordings of Josh Decker's interrogations, and showed the video tape of Josh with Miss Meeks in the grocery store. He also played the recordings of Anthony Micelli's interrogations and showed the video tape of him driving the taxi with Miss Meeks in it. When he was done and had answered their questions, he sat back in his chair to wait.

After a few minutes Officer Weston spoke, "I think we'd like to speak with your Mr. Decker."

"I'll have Millie locate his attorney. He won't talk without him."

"Who is the attorney?" Cotton asked.

"Man calls himself, Adam Saxon, Esquire."

Cotton looked at Weston both men said, "Luigi's man."

Weston said to Buck, "Yes, please round him up, he should definitely be present."

Buck picked up his phone and buzzed Millie, "Will you find Adam Saxon? We'll want the interrogation room set up for our friends from the Federal government."

"Get right on it," Millie responded, and then she switched to an outside line.

"Can I interest you in some lunch while we wait? Mr. Saxon has not proved the most cooperative."

The men nodded. They all rose and then walked from Buck's office. Buck stopped at the desk to let Millie know where they were going.

The men walked down the two blocks to the Oak Grove Cafe. Buck was greeted as usual by staff and customers alike. When they were seated and had ordered, Buck filled the two men in on how Saxon liked to call the shots, so Buck had been deliberately late for interrogations, putting the man at a disadvantage. The two men liked the plan so the three of them enjoyed a leisurely lunch. When they returned as Buck had predicted, Saxon was pacing in the front office.

"It's about time," he growled, "You'd think a person didn't have anything to do but wait on your whims."

"Mr. Saxon, if you would come with us please," Buck said cordially. To Millie he said, "Please have Mr. Decker brought to interrogation room one."

Buck led the way to the interrogation room. He held the door and allowed the others to enter. Once everyone was in the room he made the introductions. "Mr. Saxon, allow me to introduce Officers Cotton and Weston. They will be asking the questions today."

"This is rather unusual," Saxon commented. He ignored the outstretched hands of the two officers.

"To the contrary, Mr. Saxon," Cotton said, "this is standard procedure when the federal government is taking over a case."

Saxon sputtered, "Why would the federal government be taking over a local breaking and entering case?"

"It seems this is more than breaking and entering. It seems your client was in Oak Grove on behalf of the Luigi family and he is an accessory to the murder of a local resident, possibly at their request."

"I think you are mistaken. My client has lived in this town for five years. Until recently he has had no run-in with the law. Isn't that so, Wise?"

Buck nodded, but remained quiet. He was here to watch and learn.

"That is all well and good," said Cotton, "But the Luigi's are the owners of the newspaper Mr. Decker runs and he has admitted to trying to find a paper they wanted that pertains to a United States Senator."

"He didn't find any paper," Saxon insisted.

"Let's hear what he has to say when he arrives."

"I'd like a moment to confer with him before the questioning begins."

"I have arranged for him to be put in the conference room across the hall until we are ready," Buck said.

"Excellent! Take me there," Saxon demanded.

Buck opened the door and led Saxon across the hall to where Josh Decker was waiting. After Saxon entered Buck closed the door and waited.

Decker asked immediately, "What does the Chief think he has on me now?"

"Shut up and listen," Saxon hissed. "There are two federal cops across the hall waiting to interrogate you."

"What!" Decker shouted.

"That's right, sonny boy, feds," smirked Saxon. "They want to tie you to the Luigi family and make a huge name for themselves."

"What am I going to do?" whined Decker.

"Tell them what they want to know. After I'll see what kind of deal they are offering."

"I'm not going back to jail."

"It's out of my hands," the lawyer said, "I can only negotiate how much time you spend there."

"You'd better negotiate as little as possible," threatened Decker.

"Let's go see what they want."

Saxon rose, walked to the door, and knocked. Buck opened the door. The door to the interrogation room was already opened. Saxon and Decker walked into the room followed by Buck.

After both men were seated, Buck hit the tape recorders and Cotton began asking questions.

"Mr. Decker, how long have you been employed by the Luigi family?"

"I'm not. They just helped me finance my newspaper."

"Then why is it Sal Luigi is the registered owner of your paper?"

"When did that happen?"

"Five years ago."

"No way!" screamed Decker, "That rat swindled me."

"When did the Luigi's ask you to find a document concerning Senator Masterson?"

"About six months ago."

"Did they seem to be pressuring you to find it?"

"No, they didn't set a time line."

"When did you suspect that there was a time line?"

"On July 8th when Tony Micelli showed up at my door."

"Are you now saying Tony Micelli was in town before he picked up Miss Meeks on July 9th?"

"Yes. He came in the day before. Some big shot sent him to find a document on Masterson."

"Was it the tip off, you'd better find the document?"

"Yes, so I started pressuring the old lady."

"Pressuring how?"

"I started following her, and telling her I wanted to know where the paper was that she had on Masterson. At first she thought I meant library stuff and started looking up articles and other junk."

"What did you do next?"

"I started following her home, to the market, and any place else she went."

"How did she happen to get into the cab with Micelli?"

"I had her spooked. I think she thought it was Butch."

"Do you know what Micelli said to her?"

"Not a clue."

"Did Micelli go with you when you went to her house on Saturday night?"

"No, he just told me to make her some tea with the stuff he had. Said I should get her to talk first. He stayed behind and drank some beer and watched my cable channels."

"How did you get Miss Meeks to let you in?"

"I went to the back door. I was carrying one of the Carolina jasmine plants. I wanted her to think I was sorry."

"Were you sorry?"

"No way! The biddy held out. I had to push my way in. I made her fix the tea herself."

"Did you know the tea was poisoned?"

"No, I thought it had something in it to make her talk."

"What happened next?"

"When she had the tea made, I made her go to the living room. She started to sip the stuff."

"Did she tell you what you wanted to know?"

"No, the last thing she said was that the paper was safe and I'd never find it."

"Keep going."

"She finished part of the tea then just stopped."

"Stopped what?"

"Moving, talking, she just stopped. Her eyes followed me for a while as I was going through stuff. I finally figured out the tea made it so she couldn't move. I left out the front door."

"Where did you go?"

"I went to my place. Tony and me, we had a few beers."

"Then what?"

"I got the idea the old lady might have left the paper at the library. Tony thought it would be fun to trash a library, so off we went."

"Did you find the paper at the library?"

"No, just that stupid cat."

"What happened when you were done at the library?"

"We went back to my place and went to bed."

"When did Mr. Micelli decide to leave town?"

"I don't know. He suggested I try to waylay the Chief and find out what he knew. Tony seemed to think he knew something and why he wouldn't talk to me."

"How did you plan to waylay the Chief?"

"I came in brandishing a gun, it was empty, I don't like guns. Anyway, I had the secretary cut off the phone lines. I thought it would bring him out and I could back him into his office and get some answers."

"What happened?"

"He wasn't in his office and he radioed he needed help at the courthouse. I put the secretary in front of me going out the front door. I thought if there were police cars going to the courthouse I could get away. I didn't get anywhere. Buck and Tom, Jr. were waiting for me."

"Have you talked to Mr. Micelli since you were arrested?"

"Nope, I figured he was long gone until they played the tape of him."

"I think we have enough for now. Mr. Saxon, Mr. Decker." The two federal officers rose. Buck turned off the tape recorder and pulled out the tape.

"I'd like a copy of that," demanded Saxon.

Cotton turned, "You'll get your copy. Where shall we have it sent?"

"Why, I'm staying at the Oak Grove Inn, it's the only place in town," sneered Saxon.

Cotton, Weston, and Buck all left the room.

Decker said to Saxon, "Can you get me some easy time?"

"I have no idea," Saxon said, "they don't seem to have a deal to put forth."

"I did what you said. I told them everything," whined Decker.

"Quit sniveling!" Saxon said angrily. "I'll do what I can." He marched to the door, opened it and walked out.

A young officer entered, placed Decker in handcuffs and walked him back to his cell.

37 BUCK LED THE two feds into his office. "Saxon is right, Oak Grove Inn is the only place in town I can put you up. There is a Su-

per 7 Motel in River City. It's a twenty minute drive, but a nice place. Just a bit bigger than we are here."

"Sounds great!" Cotton said. "Don't relish the thought of staying in the same place as Saxon. Do like having him close at hand though, Chief."

"Let me call and see if they have rooms open." Buck picked up the phone and made the call. When he hung up he said, "They will hold two rooms for you. Millie can give you a map on your way out."

"Thanks," they said in unison.

Millie came in a few minutes later. "Well, they seem okay."

"They are the good guys. They sure got more out of Decker than I did. I think he's scared of doing hard time."

"Do you think they will give him a break?"

"Only if they can actually get something on the Luigi's."

"Well, Buck, if you don't mind, I think I'm going on home."

"Go ahead, Millie, I won't be much longer."

Millie left his office and a few minutes later Buck heard her leave the building. Buck listened to the silence for a moment, and then started closing up his office. It had been a day and he was ready to go home.

38 THE NEXT MORNING two well rested federal officers showed up in Buck's office.

Cotton did the speaking, "We'd like to meet with your prosecuting attorney and the state attorney. We need to see how best to approach Silverman. We also need to let them proceed with the charges against Decker."

Buck picked up his phone and buzzed Millie. When she picked up he said, "See if Tom, Sr. and the state's attorney are available for the federal officers."

"Sure thing, Buck," Millie said and disconnected him and picked up an outside line.

Several minutes later, Buck's phone rang Millie told him that Tom, Sr. would see them as soon as they could get there. He thanked her and hung up the phone.

"Well, it seems that we can get in as soon as we can get over to the courthouse."

The two men rose and the three of them set out for the courthouse. It was a quick walk across the street.

On arriving, the men were led into a conference room. The secretary returned a few minutes later with a cart laden with fruit, pastries, and coffee.

"Looks like they plan for us to be here a while," Buck commented. "You might as well help yourselves." Buck walked to the table and helped himself to pastries and coffee. Weston joined Buck and Cotton just poured himself a cup of coffee.

They had just settled into seats when Tom Haliday, Sr. walked into the room with another man that Buck assumed was the state attorney. Buck stood and shook hands with Tom and said, "I'd like to introduce Officers Robert Cotton and James Weston, who are assigned to the organized crime task force."

Tom shook hands with both men and turned to introduce the man with him, "This is the state's attorney, Allen Stevens." Again, the men all shook hands.

Tom cleared his throat and began their meeting, "Gentlemen, we seem to have uncovered quite a mess here in our little town. I believe you are all up to date on what Buck has done to solve this case. Are there any questions at this point?"

Robert Cotton was the first to speak, "We understand what law enforcement has done. We are most grateful to you Chief Wise for having the foresight to make duplicate copies of all interrogations and the video clips you uncovered. What we want to know is what charges you intend to bring against Josh Decker?"

"It would seem, Mr. Decker has done a fair bit of mischief. He will be charged with two counts of breaking and entering, one count of attempted kidnapping, which under the Homeland Security Act, is a felony and one count of accessory to murder," Stevens replied.

"How much jail time will he be looking at?" asked Weston.

"With his history, he is looking at twenty-five years to life."

"Is there any room for a plea or lesser sentence?"

It was the first time Buck heard Weston speak and he was impressed with the types of questions he was asking.

Stevens thought for a moment, "I suppose there is always room for a plea arrangement; it would depend on what he has to offer in return. He is not a newcomer to the prison system."

"Thank you," was all he said.

"What about our friend, Anthony Micelli?" Cotton asked.

"He would be charged with one count of joy riding, and which would probably be dropped in view of his other charges. He would also be charged with one count of breaking and entering and one count of premeditated murder," Stevens said. "He is also a second-time offender."

Cotton spoke, "He has been a small-time hood since he was a teen, this is habitual for him."

"Again, how much time are we looking at?" Weston asked.

"I'd say the murder alone will get him life without parole."

"Again, I will ask about plea bargaining."

"I would guess, at the risk of repeating myself, there is always a chance. What would you be hoping to get from this man?"

Weston looked at Cotton before continuing, "We need the name of the person who sent him to Oak Grove. With the name we would have the true killer. I'd like to see him get some kind of break if he can give us that."

Tom spoke up, "If he gives you that name, wouldn't it just make him an accessory to murder?"

"I could see it that way," Stevens agreed. "Then like Decker, he would be looking at twenty-five to life."

"Those are my questions," said Weston. "Thank you, gentlemen," he rose and shook hands all around. Cotton followed his lead.

Buck said, "Just one more thing."

Everyone turned to look at him and he continued, "I'd like to think Decker has given us everything he knows, so I'd recommend he stay at twenty-five years to life."

"We'll do what we can, Buck," said Tom. "Miss Emily was a friend of mine, too."

They all shook hands and left the room. Cotton and Weston joined Buck going back to the police station.

Cotton asked, "Do you think we can get Micelli's lawyer in?"

Buck smiled, "I thought you might want to see him, so I left instructions for Millie to call him as soon as we left for the courthouse."

"Well, done, Wise, well done," said Weston with feeling.

39 MILLIE HAD PUT Silverman and Micelli in an interrogation room. She'd seen to it they both had coffee to drink. When the three men entered, she handed Buck the recording of Decker from the night before.

Buck led the way to the interrogation room. He held the door for the other two men and entered behind them.

Silverman stood and introduced himself, "Marcus Silverman, attorney for Mr. Micelli." He held out his hand.

144

Each of the two officers shook hands with him. As Buck shook his hand he said, "This is Officer Robert Cotton and his partner Officer James Weston, they are with the federal organized crime task force."

"Pleased, I'm sure."

Cotton took over the questioning as he had the day before. Buck turned on the two tape recorders.

"Mr. Micelli, we have just come from a meeting with the local prosecutor and the state's attorney, you are looking at life without parole for your part in the murder of Emily Meeks."

"I didn't kill the old lady. Decker killed her."

"Chief Wise, would you be kind enough to play the tape from our interview with Decker yesterday?"

"Sure," said Buck as he started the tape.

"When did you suspect there was a time line?"

"On July 8th when Tony Micelli showed up at my door."

"Are you now saying Tony Micelli was in town before he picked up Miss Meeks on July 9th?"

"Yes. He came in the day before. Some big shot sent him to find a document on Masterson."

"Was it the tip off the you'd better find the document?"

"Yes, so I started pressuring the old lady."

"Pressuring how?"

"I started following her, and telling her I wanted to know where the paper was that she had on Masterson. At first she thought I meant library stuff and started looking up articles and other junk."

"What did you do next?"

"I started following her home, to the market, and any place else she went."

"How did she happen to get into the cab with Micelli?"

"I had her spooked. I think she thought it was Butch."

"Do you know what Micelli said to her?"

"Not a clue."

"Did Micelli go with you when you went to her house on Saturday night?"

"No, he just told me to make her some tea with the stuff he had. Said I should get her to talk first. He stayed behind and drank some beer and watched my cable channels."

"How did you get Miss Meeks to let you in?"

"I went to the back door. I was carrying one of the Carolina jasmine plants. I wanted her to think I was sorry."

"Were you sorry?"

"No way! The biddy held out. I had to push my way in. I made her fix the tea herself."

"Did you know the tea was poisoned?"

"No, I thought it had something in it to make her talk."

"What happened next?"

"When she had the tea made, I made her go to the living room. She started to sip the stuff."

"Did she tell you what you wanted to know?"

"No, the last thing she said was the paper was safe and I'd never find it."

"Keep going."

"She finished part of the tea then just stopped."

"Stopped what?"

"Moving, talking, she just stopped. Her eyes followed me for a while as I was going through stuff. I finally figured out the tea made it so she couldn't move. I left out the front door."

"Where did you go?"

"I went to my place. Tony and me, we had a few beers."

"Then what?"

"I got the idea the old lady might have left the paper at the library. Tony thought it would be fun to trash a library, so off we went."

"Did you find the paper at the library?"

"No, just the stupid cat."

"What happened when you were done at the library?"

"We went back to my place and went to bed."

"When did Mr. Micelli decide to leave town?"

"I don't know. He suggested I try to waylay the Chief and find out what he knew. Tony seemed to think he knew something and why he wouldn't talk to me."

"How did you plan to waylay the Chief?"

"I came in brandishing a gun, it was empty, I don't like guns. Anyway, I had the secretary cut off the phone lines. I thought it would bring him out and I could back him into his office and get some answers."

"What happened?"

"He wasn't in his office and he radioed he needed help at the courthouse. I put the secretary in front of me going out the front door I thought if there were police cars going to the courthouse I could get away. I didn't get anywhere. Buck and Tom, Jr. were waiting for me."

"Have you talked to Mr. Micelli since you were arrested?"

"Nope, I figured he was long gone until they played the tape of him."

When the taped stopped, Cotton asked, "Is there anything in that tape recording you'd care to dispute?"

Micelli looked dejected as he said, "No, that's pretty much what happened. The lady got quite a scare when she learned I wasn't the usual cabbie."

"What did you say to her while you were in the cab?"

"I just told her if she wanted to see her next birthday, she'd give over the papers about Masterson. She had the nerve to say the papers were private and her property. She looked real smug."

"Did you have any idea what was in the papers?"

"Nope, just knew I was supposed to get them whatever way I could."

"Did you tell Mr. Decker that the tea was poisoned?"

"No, didn't think the fool would have her make him some too. Guess I'm lucky he didn't drink it."

"I'd guess you are," Cotton said, "Will you tell me who sent you after the paper?"

"What's in it for me?"

"The murder charge become accessory to murder and life without parole becomes twenty-five years to life."

"I need to talk to my attorney before I say anything else."

"Fine," Cotton replied.

Buck turned off the tape recorders and retrieved the tape of Micelli. Then the three men left the room. All three watched the two men from behind a two-way mirror.

"Don't you wish you could hear them?" Buck asked.

"Nope, they are just going to argue. Silverman will want him to keep his mouth shut and Micelli will want to give up the big man," answered Weston.

Cotton just leaned against a wall and closed his eyes. Buck said nothing. It was time to wait.

The wait was over soon. Weston said, "Looks like we're going to know the result sooner than I thought."

Silverman walked to the door. He spoke to the officer standing outside. The three men took their cue and returned to the interrogation room.

Once inside, Buck began the tapes.

Silverman spoke, "My client has refused to follow my counsel. He would like something in writing which guarantees he does not serve life without parole."

Cotton said he would have the documents drawn up in the morning. He pulled a small writing tablet out of his pocket and handed it to Micelli along with a pen. "Please write the name of the person or persons who hired you to come to Oak Grove in search of documents regarding Senator Sam Masterson."

"I don't need to write it down. Senator Masterson hired me. He said the old lady had some papers which could ruin him if they got into the wrong hands."

"Did he happen to say whose hands were the wrong hands?"

"He said he had a falling out with Gino Luigi and Gino was trying to get something on him."

"Had the Senator worked with Luigi in the past?"

"Sure, it was Gino Luigi who gave the Senator the seed money for his company. They had known each other in college. Gino was the smart one so the Don sent him to college to learn business."

"Do you know how he met Senator Masterson?"

"Yeah, Masterson had an eye for the young girls and Gino used to find young girls for him. After Gino graduated they kept in touch. It's how Masterson got the job teaching in the East."

"How did Gino learn about Emily Meeks?"

"The story goes after Masterson started to become successful he and Gino took a trip to Europe. They were looking for new investments. Anyways on the trip they got into drinkin' and one thing led to another. Masterson confesses to an indiscretion with one of his students and complained to Gino it was costing him a bundle. Gino offered to have the girl taken out, but Masterson had a soft spot for her and said no. It was never mentioned again until they had a falling out."

"Do you know what the falling out was about?"

"Oh, yeah. Masterson has become this real heavy hitter on breaking up organized crime. Gino is organized crime. The two have argued about it for a long time. It came to a head when Masterson told Gino he was no longer welcome in his home as it reflected badly on his image."

"I can see where this would anger Gino."

"Well anyways, Gino remembers this thing Masterson had with his student and starts looking for all the girls who took Masterson's class the last year. He finds most of them and can't find any of them have any secrets. When they are asked about Masterson, they all say how wonderful he is."

"How did Gino find Emily Meeks?"

"That's the funny thing. Her name never showed up. It wasn't on his class list or anything. He finds out about her because one of the girls was jealous of this girl in her class who met with Masterson every week. Couldn't understand it, cuz the girl was a real brain."

"Did the girl give Gino Emily Meeks name?"

"No. Said she never saw the girl on campus again until just before Masterson left. She saw the girl leave Masterson's office one afternoon and she was surprised that the girl was pregnant. Said she always thought of her as a real meek person. Gino starts looking through all the yearbooks for the last year. He comes across Emily Meeks, laughed about the name and then sent people to check her out."

Cotton looked at Buck and asked, "Did Miss Meeks mention to anyone someone had been here asking her questions?"

"If she mentioned it to anyone it would have been her attorney Ben Wallace."

"I'll want to talk to him when we're done here," Cotton said. To Micelli he said, "Is there anything else you can tell me?"

"Yeah, Gino sent me to check on Masterson and Masterson hired me to find the paper. He told me the lady's name. I reported back to Gino and then took my time heading out here. I was getting paid by the day and expenses."

"Did Gino mention he already knew the name?"

"He said he had someone on it, but no progress was bein' made and if I could speed it up he'd be happy."

"So, both Luigi and Masterson were paying you to find Emily Meeks."

"Yeah, but Gino, he just wanted the paper and Masterson wanted her gone."

"Are you telling me even if Miss Meeks had turned over the paper to you, you would have killed her?"

"It's what I was bein' paid for."

"Did you know Josh Decker was Gino's person here?"

"No, I scoped out the town for a day. I was really here July 7th. I was pokin' around when I stumbled on to old Josh. He made killin' the old lady easy."

"Thank you, Mr. Micelli, you've been a big help," Cotton said. "I'll have the prosecutor get those papers to your attorney."

The interrogation ended and Buck turned off the tape recorders. He handed a copy of the interview to Silverman and carried the other two tapes out with him as he left. In the front office, he handed the other tape to Weston. The men shook hands and walked toward the door.

At the door Cotton turned, "Breakfast at the Oak Grove Cafe, 8 a.m. our treat."

"I'll be there," said Buck.

Silverman left the building shortly after. He did not stop at the desk, he just walked by and kept going.

40

BUCK WAS RIGHT on time for breakfast. He joined the two federal officers.

"Well, I guess you're done here."

"Almost," said Cotton. "We have a couple of things to tie up."

Buck raised an eyebrow. "Oh?"

"Your prosecutor and the state's attorney can handle Decker and Micelli. We have some bigger fish to fry," Weston said. "We'd like to keep you on board."

"Sure, anything I can do to help."

"Well, it's like this," said Cotton, "we try to keep a low profile. So, we need you to be the one who makes the arrests and gets the press."

"Just tell me what to do."

The three men hatched out their plan over breakfast. When the meal was over the two federal officers left for their hotel in River City and Buck walked back to his office.

Buck picked up the phone and made a call home.

Ruth's cheery voice greeted him, "Hello."

"Hello yourself," Buck said. "How do you feel about an out of state vacation?"

"Sure, when do you want to go?" she asked.

"Is tomorrow too soon?"

"Well, no, I guess not," she stammered. "Are we taking the boys?"

"I don't think it would be a good idea," he said.

"Oh, let me guess, I am just the decoy."

"Caught me again," he said with a chuckle.

"I'll call my parents and see if I can drop the boys off this afternoon. By the way, where are we going?"

"Didn't I mention it?" Buck asked smiling. "We're going to the Big Apple."

"New York?" Ruth was incredulous.

"That's the one. Bring something fancy, I might want to show you off."

"Oh, you," she said blushing. "I'll be ready."

Buck said good-bye and hung up the phone. Then he picked it up again and buzzed Millie. "Can you come in here for a minute?"

"On my way," she said and hung up the phone.

When Millie came in, Buck asked her to sit down. Once she was seated he went over the plan with her. He would be gone for a few days and would be putting Tom, Jr. in charge. She would not be able to reach him unless it was a dire emergency and then she could call him on his cell phone. When he finished, he asked if she had any questions.

"Do you still want to keep young Bobby Wilbur as a deputy?"

"His job is not over until Dewey is reinstated at the library or it is decided that Bobby can keep him."

"Okay."

Buck closed-up his office and headed for home to help his wife pack. He knew the federal boys were picking them up bright and early in the morning.

41 THE DRIVE TO the airport was a quiet one. Ruth leaned against Buck's shoulder and slept. The three men were deep in thought.

At the airport, they had no problem getting on the plane. The federal boys had secured a private plane. They were not required to go through security. Once in the air the two federal officers were very talkative. Each told Ruth some of the things she might want to do. Cotton had made a call to his wife and she had said she'd be happy to show Ruth some of the better places to shop and pamper herself.

Ruth was pleased that she would not have to navigate the city by herself. Although she had packed a couple of novels, she did not relish spending all of her time cooped up in a motel room.

The flight was soon over and they all went to the waiting cars. Ruth and Buck were taken to a hotel and Cotton and Weston were taken to their offices to get the proper paperwork in order.

Cotton had told Buck about a wonderful Italian place just down the block from the hotel. It was called, Robelli's. Buck had called to make reservations while Ruth was in the shower.

It was a warm night and there were quite a few people strolling along the street. Buck took Ruth's hand in his and they walked to the restaurant.

Robelli's was everything and more. It had an old-world ambiance making dining even enjoyable. Their waiter brought them a wonderful Barolo red wine and they ordered an antipasto salad, Ruth had a risotti covered in mushrooms, it is a rice dish and Buck ordered an agnolotti, a pasta made from eggs and stuffed with pork, parmesan cheese, eggs and herbs. The waiter also brought them some panettone, warm bread. The meal was served in courses, they chose to pass on dessert, but did have coffee to end their meal. They left feeling like they need never eat again and made their way back to the hotel.

When they arrived back at the hotel they stopped at the front desk for messages. There were two. One was for Ruth from Valerie Cotton, saying she would call Ruth from the hotel lobby at 10 a.m. The other was from Weston saying he would pick Buck up in the lobby at 9:30 a.m.

"I can see we have a busy day tomorrow," Buck commented. Then he turned to ask the desk clerk what time the hotel restaurant opened for breakfast.

"They open at 6:30, sir."

"Thanks," he said then turned and walked with Ruth to the elevators.

Once in their room Ruth asked, "What if we do something decadent?"

Amused Buck asked, "What did you have in mind?"

"Let's order room service and have breakfast on the balcony. The view is breath taking, she said as she walked out onto the balcony.

Buck poured them both drinks from the in-room bar. As he walked out to join Ruth on the balcony and hand her a drink he asked, "So how does 8 a.m. sound?"

"Eight! Sounds absolutely wonderful!"

"I'll go call and put in our order." Buck walked back inside and called room service to place an order. When he turned to rejoin Ruth, he discovered she had come back inside.

"What's the matter?"

She twirled the liquid in her glass and asked, "Is what you are doing here dangerous?"

"No, I'm not doing that much. My big job will be to put the handcuffs on the bad guys and talk to the press."

"You're sure?"

"I'm sure," he said as he put down his drink and walked toward his wife. When he got to her, he folded her into his arms. "If I thought I'd be in danger, I'd be here alone. Now, let's call it a night."

She looked into his eyes and kissed him. They called it a night.

42 BUCK LEFT THE room at nine. Ruth was getting in the shower. He made sure the Do

Not Disturb sign was on the door. Weston was a bit early. He found Buck reading the 'New York Times.'

"Hope this wasn't too early for you."

"Nope, I slept in until 7:30, which is a treat."

"So, what is your wife going to do today?"

"Mrs. Cotton is coming by at ten to pick her up and take her shopping."

"Good, Val will see she has a good time."

"I appreciate it. I don't have to worry about her being lost in the city or stuck in the room."

Weston led the way to his car and the two men drove off. On the way Weston pointed out some of the places worth seeing in New York.

"So, what's the big plan for today?" Buck asked.

"We are going to try to take down both men at the same time. It seems the Senator is in his New York office this week. Gino Luigi is here in his accounting firm."

"Sounds like a plan."

"Which one do you want to arrest the most?"

"Personally, I want to take down Masterson, but I'll go where you need me."

"Well, I'm sure Rob will take it into consideration."

It took close to twenty minutes for them to get to the federal offices. Once inside Buck was given a special badge to wear identifying him as a guest. They made their way to a conference room. Buck was given a cup of coffee and they sat down. Officer Cotton came in and the meeting began.

"Chief Buck Wise from Oak Grove, Michigan has joined us today. He is the reason we are able to bring down Gino Luigi and Senator Sam Masterson. We have a connection between the men going back to college days. We also have Masterson on a murder for hire charge. The plan is to take both men at the same time. When we enter the buildings, the media will be notified of arrests being made in both places. We will keep the two men in their offices long enough for the media to arrive. Chief Wise will be the arresting officer for Senator Masterson and Ike Brown will be the arresting officer for Gino Luigi. Are there any questions?"

Buck looked around until his eyes fell on Ike Brown, he was a Black man who stood about six foot six. Buck knew he would be a formidable opponent. Brown nodded.

"Who's talking to the media?"

"Ike will handle the media at Luigi's. He has worked for years to find something on them. He knows just what to say."

"Are you doing Masterson?"

"No, I'm leaving Chief Wise to handle the media surrounding the arrest of Senator Masterson. The person who was killed lived in Oak Grove. I think this one is best left to him. Are there any further questions? If not, let's get to our cars and get this done today."

The men filed out of the room. Each man was handed a bullet proof vest and a jacket that said FBI. Buck put his on and followed Weston out of the building.

"You'll be riding with Cotton," Weston said. "I have the Luigi detail. Good luck."

"Thanks, you too."

Buck waited until Cotton came out of the building. Cotton motioned him toward a car. Buck jogged over and hopped in the passenger side. The car rolled out.

"Nervous?" Cotton asked.

"No," Buck replied, "used to do this kind of thing in Detroit." It was the first time Cotton had tried to make small talk.

"How'd you end up in Oak Grove?"

"I grew up there. I wanted my boys to have a safer life than what I could give them living in Detroit."

"Makes sense."

"You got any kids?"

"We had one," Cotton said sadly, "she died of leukemia."

"I'm sorry," said Buck.

"I'm trying to convince Valerie to try again. Was hoping your wife would talk about your boys and get her thinking."

"If anyone can, it's Ruth." Buck sat quietly for a moment then said, "We lost a little girl, too. She was a preemie."

"Sorry," said Cotton.

"Maybe Ruth can convince your wife to try again. I finally did. The boys came after."

They were silent for the rest of the ride. The cars were all parked within two blocks of the Eco-World office building. Twelve men in FBI jackets converged on the building and one car headed toward the lower level parking garage. They entered the building quietly.

The receptionist looked up and saw them. Cotton motioned her to be quiet. He held a piece of paper in front of her and said, "Tell me how to get to the Senator's office."

"I can buzz up and let him know you're coming."

"NO!" said Cotton forcefully, "ask your security person to come to the front of the building."

She did as she was told and the head of security came immediately to the front. Cotton appointed someone to stay with the receptionist, and gave the orders no calls were to be put through. The security officer led them quietly up the elevator and into a hall leading to the Senator's private office. He tapped on the door.

"Come in," said the voice from the other side.

The security guard was pushed aside and Cotton pushed through the door followed by Buck and two other agents.

"What is the meaning of this?" the Senator demanded.

Cotton responded, "FBI, sir, here on a warrant." He nodded to Buck.

Buck took out his cuffs and walked toward Masterson. "Put your hands on your head," he said calmly.

"Just what is the meaning of this?"

Buck stepped behind him and placed one wrist in a cuff and then the other at the same time he said, "You are under arrest for the murder of Emily Meeks. You have the right to remain silent. Anything you say can and will be used against you in a court of law. You have the right to an attorney. If you cannot afford one, the court will appoint one to represent you. Do you understand these rights as they have been read to you?"

"Emily Meeks, who on earth is Emily Meeks?"

"I can't imagine you would forget the woman who bore your child and got you to pay her monthly for most of her life. Who took the money you paid her and bought almost half the shares to your company," Buck said.

"I'm sure I have no idea what you are talking about. This has been a mistake. I want to speak to this Meeks woman."

"That will be hard to do, Senator, your flunky killed her."

As he was escorted out of the hall he yelled to his secretary, "Get Marcus Silverman on the phone. I need him here at once."

Buck chuckled and said, "I'm afraid he is tied up in Michigan with one of your associates."

"Hrrmph," was all that Masterson could manage.

They all descended in the elevator. When they arrived on the first floor there were several members of the press on hand. Many snapped pictures and some had video cameras running.

"Senator Masterson, do you have a comment?"

"Can you tell us what this is all about?"

Cotton took Masterson out of the way and left Buck to make a statement.

"Senator Samuel Masterson was arrested this morning and charged with the murder for hire of Miss Emily Meeks, a librarian in Oak Grove, Michigan," Buck said.

"Who was Emily Meeks to the Senator?"

"She had been one of his college students."

"Why would he want her dead?"

"He raped her while she was his student and forced her to continue in a relationship with him."

"Why didn't she speak up years ago?"

"Where is she now?"

"Miss Meeks was young and frightened. She kept quiet for thirty years. In spite of her silence, Senator Masterson had her murdered." Buck paused then said, "That's all I can tell you for now."

"And who are you, sir?"

"Chief Buck Wise."

"Where are you from Chief? What is your interest in this?"

"I'm from Oak Grove, Michigan. My interest in this is justice."

Buck left the crowd of reporters each trying to scoop the other and walked out into the sunshine. Cotton waited outside for him.

"You did a nice job. It was good you could keep her daughter out of it."

"Yeah, I'm sure those vultures will be onto her soon enough."

"Let's get out of here."

SECRETS

The two men got into Cotton's car and drove to the federal building. There they dictated reports and wrapped up the paperwork. At noon television sets were brought into the conference room. The news showed first the Senator being led from his office building in handcuffs and Buck's statement. This was followed by Gino Luigi being led from his building in cuffs and Ike Brown's statement that Gino was being charged with racketeering and conspiracy to commit murder. Neither of the men had comments to make. There was applause all around. Ike and Buck both received pats on the back. Then people broke up and went back to work.

Weston and Cotton took Buck to lunch at a little deli they knew about. It was past time for the regular lunch crowd so they knew they would be able to enjoy their sandwiches.

Weston and Cotton were regulars so the proprietor began making their sandwiches. It was so hard for Buck to choose that he just took the house special on dark rye. It was the hugest sandwich he had ever seen and the most delicious. He had them wrap half of it to take with him.

"Nice work today, Buck," said Cotton. "I expect you will be bombarded with press for the next couple of days. Our prosecutor will want a statement from you. In the meantime, here are a couple of tickets to a show. You and your wife have a good time."

"Thanks."

"I'll drive you back to the hotel," Weston said.

"Okay." Buck couldn't remember when he'd felt so speechless.

In the car Weston said, "I want to thank you for letting us come into your town and take over."

"I was glad to do it. I didn't know how I was going to get anything else out of either one of them."

"Most local officers don't like us coming in, but you didn't seem to resent us."

"I stumbled on to something out of my league. I'm glad to have the help. You're welcome to come back any time."

"I'll remember that," said Weston as the car pulled up to the curb.

43

BUCK AND RUTH spent the rest of the week enjoying the sight and sounds of New York City. The show tickets Cotton had given him were for "Chicago." Buck took Ruth to trendy Glitter. The restaurant was all they expected and more. For their first course they had the corn and clam chowder as an appetizer, their entrée was roast prime rib, with broccoli stuffed baked potatoes, and finally for dessert they had crème brulee, after they went to see "Chicago." They finished off the evening with a carriage ride through Central Park. Buck also spent time on local TV shows and giving interviews to reporters. They had amassed a collection of newspaper articles to take back home with them.

Weston arrived on the morning they were to leave to give them a ride to the airport. Again, they would be flying on a private jet. The two men shook hands and Buck and Ruth got ready to board the plane.

"Mrs. Wise," Weston said, "I really want to thank you for spending time with Val."

Confused Ruth said, "She was a wonderful tour guide."

"I talked to her last night and she told me, she and Rob were going to try to have another baby. I want to thank you."

"You're welcome," said Ruth more puzzled than ever.

Weston looked at Ruth's face and laughed, "I'm sorry, I thought you knew. Val is my twin sister."

Ruth took a good look at James Weston then she too started to laugh. "I guess I wasn't being very observant."

"No problem. But thanks for talking to her. She's been real depressed these last couple of years. I know this will be good for her." He looked at Buck then said, "Have a safe trip."

The flight home was uneventful. Ruth and Buck were glad to be home. Neither one of them was prepared for the sight that greeted them. The whole town had turned out, balloons were flying, the high school band was playing, and leading everyone were Ben Wallace and Ella Mitchell. They were given a parade through town to the park.

Once people were all gathered in the park, Tom, Sr. banged a drum to get everyone's attention. "I think we should ask our Chief to give a speech."

The crowd must have agreed as there were overwhelming cheers and calls of "We want Buck. We want Buck."

Buck found an empty picnic table to stand on and looked at his friends and neighbors. When he found his voice, he said, "I have done nothing special, just my job. I thank you for all of this." He stepped down.

Seth Rankin said from somewhere in the crowd, "Enough with the speech makin' let's eat."

Everyone laughed and they broke up into groups and made their way to the tables. All the tables were loaded with food. Ruth's parents were there with the boys but said they would bring them home in the morning. The town partied well into the next morning. A good time was had by all. Even Mrs. Wilkes had her say when she found Buck sitting at one of the tables.

"Glad ya got the job done."

"Thank you, Mrs. Wilkes."

Buck and Ruth made their way home by about one in the morning. As the got ready for bed Ruth said, "So how does it feel to be a hero?"

"I'm not a hero, just a guy doing his job." He quietly turned out the light.

44

THINGS IN OAK Grove settled down to normal. There were kids drag-racing out on the old plank road to be dealt with. Seth Rankin still stumbled home most Friday nights after he got paid. Yes, life was normal.

The town counsel met to see about hiring a librarian. Mrs. Watkins from the high school said that she would finish out the summer doing the job, but they needed to find someone permanent by the time school opened. It was agreed and they placed an advertisement in the new town paper and one in River City.

It was about this time that Millie asked for a couple of weeks off. Said she was going to take a trip out of town. She was very mysterious about it, but Buck gave her the time and she left. Betty Sue and her manicure set moved in to help out.

The trial of Josh Decker would start next week unless he agreed to the plea bargain. Buck was sure he didn't see twenty-five to life as a bargain. Anthony Micelli had taken his offer and been transferred to the federal penitentiary in Milan. Buck was glad he was gone.

It seemed like no time at all and Millie was back. She picked up right where she left off. It was then things started getting strange at the police department. Flowers started arriving daily and mysterious packages started arriving for Millie. Millie got personal phone calls at work, something she had never done before. She also seemed to daydream a lot.

Buck commented to Ruth one evening as they sat in their backyard, "Ever since Millie came back the office has looked like a flower shop. She's getting some strange packages too. I find her looking off in space like some dreamy-eyed teenager."

"What's so strange about a man sending flowers and packages to someone he likes?"

"What do you mean? Millie isn't seeing anyone."

"No one in Oak Grove you mean."

"What do you mean no one in Oak Grove? Where else would Millie be seeing someone?"

Ruth walked into the house chuckling. Over her shoulder she said, "It's not for me to say."

"Women," said Buck and he settled in his chair to watch the moon rise.

45 IT WAS THE week before Labor Day. There were lots of people in town. The holiday brought in all kinds of tourists and relatives. The weather was even cooperating. The phone rang in the front office. The next thing Buck heard was Millie shriek. Buck jumped up and ran to the front office. There was Millie with the phone in her hand staring across the room at James Weston.

"Weston, nice to see you," Buck said hoping Millie would recover from her speechlessness. "Won't you come in and chat for a minute?"

"I'd like to, Buck."

As he walked across the room he winked at Millie. She quickly put down the phone and busied herself at her desk. Buck caught the wink, but it didn't register with him.

As Weston sat down, Buck asked, "What brings you back so soon?"

"Well, I was wondering if you had any openings in your department."

"You wanting to apply?"

"If there is an opening, I kinda thought I might want to settle in a place like this."

"I do believe I could find an opening if you're serious. It won't pay what you get with the feds."

"How soon could I start?"

"How soon would you be wanting to start?"

"I'm not sure can I get back to you in a minute or two?"

"Sure," Buck said suspiciously.

Weston got up and walked to the door of Buck's office. In three strides, he was at Millie's desk.

Buck got to his office door just in time to see Weston go down on one knee. He didn't have to hear to know what Weston was asking Millie. It explained the flowers and packages which had adorned his office for a month. He also didn't need to be a mind reader to see what Millie's answer was. She threw her arms around Weston and almost knocked them both over. Buck retreated to his office.

Buck quietly placed a call home.

"Hello," he heard Ruth's cheery voice on the other end.

"Hello, yourself," said Buck "you'd better clear your schedule I think you're going to be needed to help plan a wedding."

"Buck Wise, what on earth are you talking about?"

"Well, it seems I'm gaining a new deputy and Millie will be changing her name."

"Jim is there? He asked her to marry him? Well, it's about time."

"You knew?" he asked incredulously.

"Of course, I knew. Unlike you men, we women talk to each other. So, get off the phone so she can call me."

Buck chuckled and hung up the phone. He marveled at how his wife could know so much more about what was going on when he prided himself on having his finger on the pulse of his town.

46 MILLIE AND JIM were married the weekend after Labor Day. Ruth was the matron of honor and Rob Cotton was the best man. Valerie Cotton was also in the wedding as were Buck and his two boys. Ben Wallace had stepped in to give the bride away. It was a simple ceremony with close friends. The reception was a barbeque in Buck's backyard. Mrs. Maxwell had outdone herself with the wedding cake.

Jim had purchased the Meeks house and was in the process of doing some restoration. The place had needed a handyman. Millie loved the gardens and had a swing put in the backyard. They were going to honeymoon in the Bahamas and had a flight to catch.

The Cotton's had an announcement to make, too. They were going to be parents in about seven months. Everyone congratulated them.

The evening wound down. Millie and Jim made their exit. Rob and Val were staying at the Oak Grove Inn so they left walking. Ella and Matt Mitchell had gone back to River City. There children had been with Matt's parents for the day. Buck got the boys settled into bed and went to help Ruth with the clean up. Clean up didn't take long as everyone had pitched in before leaving.

"One thing I don't get," Buck started, "how did you know there was a romance going on with Millie and Jim?"

"Millie told me."

"But when did it start?"

"When he and Rob first came to town, he called Millie from his cell phone that first night as they were going to River City. He asked her if she could come by the motel and pick him up and show him the best place for dinner."

"How did I miss all this?"

"It seems you were busy solving a murder," Ruth chuckled.

They finished putting chairs away and stood on their patio watching the moon rise.

"This is a nice way to end the summer," Ruth said.

"It sure is."

"I'm sorry Emily Meeks died, but I'm glad Millie met Jim and we met the Cottons."

"I'm sorry about Miss Emily, too," said Buck, "I'm sure she would be happy with the way things turned out."

"I'm sure she would."

They turned out the lights and headed to bed.

EPILOGUE

Five years later

OAK GROVE WAS still the sleepy little town, tucked away in an old oak grove, which it had always been. Buck Wise had been the Chief for eleven years. As he drove through town on this sultry summer evening he reflected on his life in this town.

Joey would be driving soon and then Jake would follow. He was proud of his sons. They both played football, basketball and baseball. Both were honor students and had plans to go to college.

The town counsel had hired Ella Mitchell to be the librarian. She and her family had moved here five years ago. Dewey had been reinstated in the library and had found himself a mate. There were several cats living in the library and keeping the mouse population down. The library also had a new children's wing, the Emily Meeks wing. There Ella held story time and did crafts with the pre-school children. She also did week-end crafts with the older children. Miss Emily would have been pleased.

Jim and Millie Weston had a little boy and a baby on the way. Millie was only working part-time at the station right now. She'd be back full-time when this new baby was getting around. As with her son, Millie would bring this new baby to work with her. Jim was working part-time as a police officer and part-time as a handyman, every once in a while, he would

169

consult for his friend, Rob Cotton. Buck thought he enjoyed the handyman stuff the most.

The Cottons came to town on such a regular basis that they bought a little place down by the river. They had twin girls who just turned five. Valerie and the girls spend the summers there. Buck thought they made a great addition to their community. He hoped they'd settle in Oak Grove permanently.

Matt Mitchell owned and operated the Oak Grove Gazette. He had made it an outstanding little paper again. He covered all the football and basketball games at Oak Grove High School, the town counsel meetings and the PTA. He even ran a police-beat. Weddings and birth announcements were also something to look forward to.

Ben Wallace retired. He spends as much time as he can at the library. He even reads on occasion for story time. Buck thought Ben saw Ella as the daughter he never had. He was sure Ben saw a young Emily every time he looked at Ella. As for Ella, she has developed a great fondness for him. Her children call him Grampa Ben and often as not are at his house rather than their own.

Ruth had found a passion. She had started writing. She started with the history of Oak Grove. The book was featured prominently at the library and was sold in every store in town. From there she went on to write about the murder of Miss Emily. The book had been a best seller in the non-fiction category. Now she was working on some children's books and had an idea for a novel. Buck had turned the unused dining room into an office for her and she spent hours at her keyboard typing away. Everyone in town was waiting for her next book. She had also surprised him four years ago by presenting him with a beautiful baby daughter. Sarah Jane was the apple of his eye. She was a green eyed, strawberry blonde who was adored by her older brothers. Buck knew he was going to have to keep his eye on her when she grew older, otherwise she'd break every heart in town.

Josh Decker finally took the plea he was offered. He is still serving twenty-five to life for his crimes in Oak Grove. He was not having it easy in prison. The last Buck heard he'd been in some-kind-of-fight and needed to be hospitalized because of his injuries. Buck had a hard time finding much sympathy for him.

Gino Luigi would be in prison for the rest of his natural life. Buck had been at his trial. He'd been called to testify about how he discovered the connection between Luigi and Masterson. Gino's business had been seized and his crime family closed-down. He had tried to run his family business from inside, but did not have the power to do so.

As Rob Cotton said, "We get one and another one is waiting to step in. It's a vicious circle." Rob had been promoted to bureau chief and spent most of his time behind a desk anymore. He spent as much of his summer as he could with Val and the girls in Oak Grove. Many were the afternoons he and Buck would go fishing.

Senator Samuel Masterson was sent to prison for life for his part in the Emily Meeks murder. Buck had testified at his trial. Ella Mitchell took over Eco-World and then sold it for millions. She did appear in court the day he was sentenced and asked to speak for the family of the victim. Her statement was simple but impassioned and the judge showed him no mercy. Buck had been proud of her. Masterson's wife divorced him, but was not able to get much in assets as they were seized by the government for his crime of racketeering. She had disappeared with his two sons. He spends his days in prison writing his memoirs.

This was one time when justice won against the bad guys. Despite the town's loss, many good things came to be. Oak Grove has survived and become a better place for having known Emily Meeks. It is exactly the kind of place where you could raise your children. Buck Wise should know he was raised there and so were his children.

ACKNOWLEDGMENTS

First, I'd like to thank my editors who have worked tirelessly to fix all my mistakes. Diane Sather, my sister, Jamie Kline, my daughter, and Donavee Vigus, my mom, all of whom are avid readers, working women, and busy homemakers. Their requests for the next chapter kept me going. Also to William Vigus, my dad, who added his two cents and a male perspective.

Special thanks go to Sheriff Howie Hanft who took a late-night call to help me with sentencing for my criminals.

I also owe thanks to my students who told me it was good and kept tabs on how many words I was writing so I could get this done.

Something should also be said about the group who started the National Novel Writing Month program. If it weren't for them, I'd still just be thinking about this novel.

ABOUT THE AUTHOR

Retired teacher Rebecka Vigus spends her time writing, reading, crocheting, hiking, and swimming. She travels seeking the ideal place to call home. Ms. Vigus has been writing since she was in her pre-teens. Since her first book, a volume of poetry entitled *Only a Start and Beyond*, she has penned eight full-length novels, one book for children, several short stories, and even a self-help book for tweens and teens. Ms. Vigus has been listed as a Michigan Author and Illustrator at the State of Michigan website.

CPSIA information can be obtained
at www.ICGtesting.com
Printed in the USA
FSHW011155121020
74657FS

9 781946 848956